his eyes, before a pleased expression settled in those mesmerizing blue depths. "That's really great, Sophia. I'll stop by the college this Friday."

"Can I go with you?" she asked. "I'd like to talk to the art teacher."

He nodded. "Of course. I'll swing by here around ten to pick you up. Or will you be at the townhouse?"

"I'll be here. Thanks. I appreciate you hooking me up."

As soon as she said it, his gaze darkened, then dropped to her lips. Damn...that was the look that always revved her engines. All her good parts instantly sparked to life, and a shiver of heat rippled down to her toes.

She didn't remember their attraction being this strong.

His smile slowly faded about the same time her heart rocked hard in her chest. They stood there, barely a foot apart, staring at each other. She didn't dare to breathe, or blink. But she knew she needed to move. Trouble was, she couldn't remember if moving away, or stepping closer was the right thing to do.

His gaze was a stormy blue, no doubt reflecting his inner turmoil. She wanted to make him feel better, but the line between what she wanted and what *he* needed began to blur.

A second later they lunged for each other.

What they're saying...

About Wyne and Dine:

"Ms. Michaels has penned another hot and steamy story for her fans to enjoy. I loved that not only is this a new series, but also some of the characters make their appearance from the Harland County Series. The author knows how to create a story that is believable and hard to put down once you start reading it.—
Night Owl Reviews, *Reviewer Top Pick*
--Finalist BTS eMagazine Red Carpet Book Award/Reader's Choice-Best Best Book

About Wyne and Chocolate:

"The Citizen Soldier series has a fantastic new addition with Wyne and Chocolate. The book had a great start. I found myself laughing out loud right away - and that set the tone for a light-hearted, funny, and romantic read. I've read a LOT of romance books, and Wyne and Chocolate has one of the best first kisses that I have read."
—Reviewer- Romancereader

About Her Uniform Cowboy:

"Ms. Michaels pens a tale with pure heart and true grit! This story will hit so many readers close to home there is not one part of the plot that will feel foreign. No super models here, just true, down to earth servicemen and woman getting back to their place in the world. The characters and plot have a wonderful arc and the laughter, tears and emotional ride readers get to take on this journey will not disappoint."
—InD'tale Magazine, Crowned Heart of Excellence
--Voted BEST COWBOY in a Book/Reader's Choice-LRC
--1st Place BTS eMag Book Awards-Best Romance
--2nd Place BTS eMag Book Awards for Best Book

About Army Ranger with Benefits

This story captured me from the first minute and a lot of the reason for that is the authors way of writing so I feel like I live the story with the characters.
What I liked:

* Good storyline
* Wonderful characters described with a lot of feelings and realistic insecurities that made them "normal" people
* No unnecessary descriptions of surroundings
* Lots of dialogues
* Fun, sad and reflective moments
* Sweet and hot love scenes
* Familiar secondary characters make the story even better because it feels like I visit family
* If I'm not mistaken there will at least be one more book in this series and I hope there will be a story for Dom (Vince's brother)

This is the fourth book in this series but they can be read as standalone although I recommend reading in order if you like to get the feeling of familiarity.
~lovinghotbooks Great 5 star ☐ read.

-- I have finally found a book-boyfriend. *swoon*
If you enjoy reading romance stories with humor, heat, and heart, with emotions that dig deep yet are not angsty, with relationships that are lasting and true, with loyal friends who always have your six, you are going to love this series. Yes, Army Ranger With Benefits is a stand-alone novel - but why miss on all the fun?!
~BooksandSpoons ~ Five Spoons!

Wine and Scenery

Also by Donna Michaels

~The Citizen Soldier Series~
(Harland County Spinoff Series)

Wyne and Dine
Wyne and Chocolate
Wyne and Song
Wine and Her New Year Cowboy
Whine and Rescue (KW)
Wine and Hot Shoes
Wine and Scenery

~Harland County Series~

Harland County Christmas (Prequel)
Her Fated Cowboy
Her Unbridled Cowboy
Her Uniform Cowboy
Her Forever Cowboy
Her Healing Cowboy
Her Volunteer Cowboy
Her Indulgent Cowboy
Her Hell Yeah Cowboy (KW)
Her Troubled Cowboy (Citizen Soldier Crossover)
Her Hell No Cowboy (KW)

~The Men of At Ease Ranch Series~
~Entangled Publications~

In An Army Ranger's Arms
Her Secret Army Ranger
The Right Army Ranger
Army Ranger with Benefits
The Army Ranger's Surprise - 07/09/18

Wine and Scenery

CITIZEN SOLDIER SERIES BOOK #7

Donna Michaels

New York Times & USA Today
Bestselling Author

Dear Sylvia,
Thanks for reading!
Love,
Donna Michaels

WINE AND SCENERY
Citizen Soldier Series/Book 7

ISBN-13: 978-1987437614
ISBN-10: 1987437616

Print edition April 2018
Book 7 in Citizen Soldier Series

Dedication

To the fans of my Citizen Soldier and Harland County series. This is a hero I've been wanting to write for a long time. I hope you enjoy.

To my wonderful husband for serving for over thirty years. Congratulations on your retirement from full time National Guard. So proud of you. Thank you for putting up with my long hours. Love you dearly!

To all the men and women who served and have served. Thank you for your sacrifice. And to your families for their sacrifices. My family thanks you.

♥

Chapter One

"So...did you say yes?"

Towel drying herself, Sophia Nardovino paused to stare at her cell phone which was set to speaker on the bathroom counter, questioning if she'd heard her mother correctly.

"Sophia? Are you there?"

"Yeah, Ma." She sighed. "Nothing's changed. I told Gino no for tenth time, and I'm still here drying off."

Her mother's *tsk* echoed through the phone. "You're too hard on that boy. What's so bad about marrying him? He comes from a good Italian family."

Unlike her mother, that wasn't one of Sophia's requirements for a husband. Nor was being a slick womanizer. Besides, she didn't want to get married just yet. She was focused on building her set design portfolio for her career.

"It's the perfect match," her mother continued. "His family is into real estate. Your family is in construction."

"Doesn't make him the right fit for me." Using her towel, she wiped the mist off the mirror of the master bath in a townhouse that used to belong to her

1

college friend's brother. Brandi told her Keiffer was now living in Harland County, Texas, near her, and insisted Sophia use the place while she was there building sets for her friend, Phoebe—a Broadway star who was opening her own theater in the Poconos.

"Why doesn't that make him right for you?"

She blinked at her mother's question, and a snort rippled up her throat. "Well, for one, he's an arrogant ladies man." Something she'd never tolerate.

"So was your father before we started dating," her mother pointed out. "You just need to give Gino a chance."

Eww.

A shudder ricocheted down her spine. "I did, Ma. Last year. Remember? I went on a date with him, because you, Dad, and Gino kept badgering me."

"Once isn't enough to get to know someone." Her mother's tone was borderline scolding.

Sophia snorted again. "Believe me, one date with Gino was too much." Bile raced up her throat at the memory.

The instant she'd opened her apartment door, she knew it was a mistake. A big one—with a slick grin and unexpected attitude to match.

But that wasn't the worst part.

"What was so wrong with the date?" her mother asked, as if Sophia hadn't told her several times already.

"The fact I couldn't breathe, for one thing." She shuddered again. "He wore so much cologne, Mrs. Switzer's cat across the hall sneezed three times."

"That's her fault for snooping."

2

Sophia lived in a well-maintained building in Queens, with nice neighbors. "Ma, her door was shut."

"Then she shouldn't have left the poor thing out in the hallway."

She shook her head. "The cat wasn't in the hallway. She was inside Mrs. Switzer's apartment...behind a closed door."

"That's still no reason not to go out with the guy again," her mother insisted.

"Yes, it is," she insisted right back. "He killed my taste buds. Everything I ate that night tasted like his cologne. Then there was the lovely stop at a club where he danced with at least three other women, while I sat and watched." Granted, that was after she'd refused to dance with him again. He'd lost that privilege after assuming it was okay to let his hands roam freely over her body.

There was only man she'd grant that privilege, but their fling was a long time ago. Ryder was probably married with several children by now.

She wondered briefly if she'd run into him while in the Poconos.

"Maybe he was trying to impress you with his moves, or something." Now, her mother was reaching.

She laughed outright. "Trust me, Ma. You would be less than impressed with his moves that night."

"What? Why?" Renata Nardovino's tone rose an octave, never a good sign. "What did he do?"

Dammit. She shouldn't have said anything.

"Nothing I couldn't handle. If it had been a problem, I would've called the guys."

3

Beyond overprotective, her three older brothers effectively scared away every single date Sophia had ever brought home while growing up. They most definitely would not have been pleased with Gino stealing a kiss at the end of their date, or the fact he'd grown extra hands, and used too much tongue.

Her reflection shook as revulsion shot down her spine. That had been nowhere close to the best kiss she'd ever received. A smile tugged her lips, and her gaze softened in the mirror as the memory of that incredible embrace washed over her.

It'd happen five years ago, right here in the Poconos, during the best New Year's Eve of her life. Sophia had spent a few days with Brandi and her family. The fact her friend had four smokin' hot older brothers was a plus, but it was a friend of one of the brothers who'd captured Sophia's attention—and much more—that week.

Not only had Ryder been an incredible kisser, he'd had a way of making her body quiver with just a look. *A look*. It was crazy. No one had done that before, or since. Although, with her domineering brothers, she'd only had three lovers, none of which her family knew anything about. Ryder had been her second, and by far, the best. The sexy National Guardsman had kind of ruined her for anyone else.

So far.

The last guy hadn't measured up, although, in truth, she'd shared quite a bit of wine with Ryder that night, so perhaps that played a part in her exuberant reactions to the man.

Yeah, that was probably it.

"Sophia? Are you still there?" Her mother's voice brought her back to the present.

"Yes, Ma, sorry. I was towel drying my hair." Which she immediately started to do, so it wasn't a complete fib.

"I asked if you ran to the Poconos to get away from my meddling?" Anxiety had crept into her mother's tone.

"No," she quickly replied. "And I didn't run away. I'm here because Phoebe asked me to help with the first few productions at her new theater, remember? You know I love working with Phoebe."

"I know you do," her mother said, sounding relieved. "And Mandy said she'd be happy to fill in for you at work."

This was a discussion Sophia already had with her sister-in-law a few days ago. The sweetheart was eager to pick up a hammer and stop answering phones for the family's multi-million dollar construction company. She always thought Mandy's talents were wasted in their office, and this was the perfect way to prove it. Plus, it helped alleviate some of Sophia's guilt for leaving on such short notice.

"I just hope I'm not the reason you left. That I didn't push you away," her mother continued.

She frowned at her reflection. "You could never do that, Ma. I love you, but I would appreciate it if you'd please stop trying to find me a husband."

"Sophia…*mio Dio*…you're twenty-nine already. I had two children by that age, and my family is my greatest joy." Her mother's tone turned wistful. "I just want that for you, too."

Although she could do without the age reminder, Sophia knew her mother wanted what she thought was best for her. "I know, Ma. And I want a family, I do—but on my terms. If you stopped finding me dates, and my brothers stopped scaring away the ones I found, I might've been married by now."

A sigh rustled through the phone. "All right, I'll back off, but if you don't have any viable prospects by the beginning of September, I'm stepping back in."

Great. A three-month reprieve.

"Thanks, Ma." Smiling, she ran a comb through her wet hair. "I should probably go and finish getting ready. I'm supposed to meet Phoebe in less than an hour."

She should probably check in with her first, though.

"Okay, dear. I'll call you tomorrow."

Before she could reply, or groan, her mother hung up.

Hopefully, she wasn't going to call every single day for the next three months.

Still, better than being in the Big Apple and under their microscope, she thought to herself as she put in her contacts. It hadn't been a total lie. Coming to the Poconos was job related, and although Sophia would do anything for her family, she also needed a break from them and their well-meaning interfering.

Other than her mother's daily phone call, though, she was pretty much free during her stay. A smile spread across her lips and an invisible weight lifted from her shoulders. There was no one around to keep tabs on her here. That brief visit, all those years ago, had instilled a sense of freedom she never forgot, another reason Sophia always longed to come back to the Poconos. It was that feeling of autonomy she desired...not the mindboggling orgasms from a certain sexy Guardsman.

Nope.

Wrapping the towel around her taller-than-average frame, she noted it barely covered her nether bits. At five feet nine inches, she was a giant compared to the females in her family. Heck, compared to some of the men, too.

With another grin on her lips, she opened the door and headed into the bedroom to get dressed. She was halfway to the closet where she'd unpacked her clothes last night, when a man walked into the bedroom.

Gasping, she stopped dead as her heart leapt into her throat.

"Oh...sorry," he stammered, halting near the door, brows lifted in shock. "Ethan didn't tell me someone was in here."

Ethan was Phoebe's husband. Sophia relaxed, not because the man knew Ethan, but because the initial shock had worn off and she recognized the intruder.

Ryder...

Damn. The years had been kind.

Still tall and lean, he seemed broader, with muscles that stretched his shirt to its limits. Memories of licking a younger version of all that lay underneath flashed through her mind, sending a flutter of awareness through her belly. She took in the way his well-worn jeans creased in the best places. And be still her heart…a tool belt hugged his trim hips. The men she worked with wore them, but none ever made her want to strip them naked.

Good Lord, he was hot.

Brown hair, worn a little longer on top and lightened by the sun, emphasized those mesmerizing, sky blue eyes she swore could see straight into her soul. He must've left the Guard, because his hair was a bit too long to be military. Without the haircut restrictions, he had a little sideburn thing going on that accentuated his perfect features and strong jaw.

The man was sexy before…now he was freaking sexy-as-hell. She knew he had a supermodel sister, but wow, he could easily grace the cover of men's magazines.

"Hello, Ryder," she finally said, realizing he was waiting for her to reply.

His head jerked back and he narrowed his gaze. "Do I know you?"

Ouch.

Disappointment rocked her heart.

"Only in the biblical sense." Shoot. When was she going to learn not to speak before running it through her brain first? But since it slipped out, she might as well own it, and squash down the disillusionment and pain ripping through her chest at the knowledge their incredible time together had only been memorable on her end. She tipped her head and held his gaze. "I'm Sophia. Brandi's friend."

Dawning straightened his brow and cleared the confusion from his eyes. "New Year's Eve." He smiled, and dammit, the transformation to friendly stole her breath. "Sorry I didn't recognize you, Sophia. You look a lot different than I remember."

True. Since their long ago…tryst, she'd gone up a cup size, pants size, and her hair was no longer short and choppy with blue streaks. Her rebellious period had long passed. Now, her hair was her natural mocha brown, one length, and fell well past her shoulders.

"Are you wearing contacts?" he asked, stepping closer.

That was her biggest difference. "Yeah." She nodded.

"Why? Your eyes were amazing."

A wave of warmth rushed through her at the compliment. "Thanks, but not so much for a freakishly tall Italian."

As if her height wasn't a tough enough cross to bear, she'd been born with heterochromia—a difference in the color of the iris. She had one brown and one blue, but with the wonderful invention of colored contacts, she now preferred to go all brown. Just like her family.

Although, surprisingly, they were always trying to get her to stop wearing them.

"Well, I thought your eyes were perfect the way they were." A smile tugged his mouth, and as his gaze dropped to her feet and slowly rose back up, she remembered the only thing covering her freshly showered body was a towel.

A too-small towel.

Heat rushed into her face, and she barely refrained from crossing her arms over her chest. Why bother? He'd seen her naked—and then some—once upon a time.

His gaze returned to hers a second before the phone in his pocket started to ring. The appreciation in his eyes disappeared as he straightened his shoulders. "Sorry for the intrusion, Sophia. I'll give you your privacy now and come back later," he said, fishing the cell from his pocket.

Nodding, she stood there, watching him leave, noting the width of his shoulders and how his torso tapered into a vee above his exceptional butt. Heat skittered through her body. It was official. His back view was nearly as gorgeous as his front.

"Seriously? They out-bid us again?" He closed the door behind him, and it muffled the rest of his conversation.

But she understood the aggravation in his tone. It sucked when you spent hours working on an estimate, trying to figure out how much you could afford to trim costs in order to secure a bid...only to have someone swoop in and steal it from you.

It had forced her father to expand their working territory in hopes of lining up more jobs. She was lucky enough to still be able to work close to home, so she could also do the occasional set design on the side, but her brothers were working the new territories, somewhere in the western part of New York.

Her gaze remained on the closed door. Ryder was a smart guy. He'd figure something out. Right now, she needed to get dressed, then find out how to get to Phoebe's.

Last night, she'd arrived too late to see her friend, so she grabbed the key Phoebe had left at the front desk, and used the outside entrance to the townhouse. But apparently, her brilliant designer friend Brandi also built in another entrance through a hallway that connected all the family townhomes to the main residence where Phoebe lived.

Must be how Ryder had gained access.

Awareness tumbled down to her toes. Stupid body. The guy wasn't even in the place anymore and yet he still had a lingering effect on her.

But it didn't matter. She wasn't in Pennsylvania to reconnect with the guy. No, she was there to work. So, despite the fact he hadn't sported a wedding ring—which she...uh...unintentionally noticed—Sophia pushed him to the back of her mind.

Her focus belonged on designing and building sets for Phoebe's summer productions. They would be a welcome addition to her resume and portfolio, before her big meeting with two Broadway producers in the fall. Her preliminary designs for a major spring musical had garnered her a callback. She had a few changes to make per their request, but she was determined to bring her A-game to that meeting. Getting distracted by a sexy fling from her past was not smart.

With a shake of her head, she pushed Ryder to the back of her mind, and quickly opened the closet. Since today was a discussion day, she slipped into a comfortable sundress and sandals, before calling Phoebe to confirm their morning meeting.

"Hi, Sophia," her friend said, a smile evident in her tone. "The front desk told me you were here."

She nodded. "Yeah, I got in late and didn't want to wake you. So, I'm checking to see if we're still on for this morning."

"Absolutely. If you're ready, why don't you come to my place now? We can look at your designs over coffee. I'm so excited," Phoebe said, all in one breath. "The main residence is through the door at the end of the hall. It's unlocked, so just come in and head down the stairs to the kitchen. You can't miss it."

Never one to pass up coffee, she agreed, before hanging up, then grabbed her laptop and purse on her way out of the townhouse.

In the hall, she passed three other doors like hers. What a great way for the Wyne family to enjoy the resort, while retaining their privacy from guests. Her friend Brandi was a genius.

Entering the main house, Sophia's admiration for her old college buddy increased as she walked down a gorgeous wooden staircase, into an open floor plan of a family room-kitchen combo. The décor was rustic and warm, with wooden floors and walls, and a huge stone fireplace, but the floor to ceiling windows were the highlight of the room. They let in a view of the lake sparking through the trees.

"Wow, this place is amazing," she said, stepping off the last step, where Phoebe greeted her with a hug.

Her friend chuckled. "I know. I'm the luckiest woman ever. I'm married to an incredible man who has an adorable son, I live in this amazing home his sister designed, and now, I get to work out of a top-notch theater that *I* get to design."

A grin tugged her lips as she drew back. "You're right. You are lucky. And, oh my God, that coffee smells divine."

"Have a seat." Smiling, Phoebe motioned toward the kitchen table. The epitome of cool and relaxed, she had her hair pulled back in a ponytail and wore a similar sundress. "I'll get us some coffee."

"Thanks." She set her purse and laptop bag on one of the chairs and couldn't help but note how content and happy the award-winning Broadway star was, playing domestic hostess. Warmth spread through Sophia's body. It was nice to see her friend so happy. "Where are Ethan and Tyler?" she asked, taking a seat.

Phoebe's husband was a guide at the resort he owned with his brothers, and Tyler was Ethan's eight-year-old son from a previous marriage.

"Ethan's working," she replied. "A couple of guests signed up for a three-hour hike. And Tyler's in Texas for the summer." Sadness crept into her friend's eyes. "He's only been gone two days, but it's weird. It feels more like two hundred."

Sophia knew the woman loved the young boy as if he were her own flesh and blood. "That's right." She nodded. "Brandi mentioned her nephew was coming to visit when we Skype'd last month. I also got to see her sweet little baby boy."

"Oh my God, I know. Isn't Kyle just the cutest?" Phoebe gushed.

"He sure is." Envy tightened her chest. *Someday.* She truly believed she'd find the right man—on her own—and have a family and a career she loved, too.

13

But not right now. She had to work on the career part first.

"Before I forget, Ethan told me Ryder is supposed to stop by your place to fix a few things." Phoebe set a delicious smelling mug of coffee in front of her, before sitting down with her own. "I heard the two of you had a little bit of history, so I thought I should warn you."

Reaching for her mug, she snorted. "Too late."

Her friend sat up straight. "He stopped by already?"

"Yep." Sophia sipped her coffee and wondered just exactly what she'd heard about her *history* with Ryder.

"So?" Phoebe leaned closer. "How'd it go?"

Another snort rippled up her throat. "Awkward." She set her coffee down and sat back in her seat. "I'm just glad I decided to wrap a towel around me when I got out of the shower."

"Oh my God...he walked in on you as you got out of the shower?"

She shook her head. "Not exactly. I entered the bedroom from the bathroom a few seconds before he entered from the living room." An image of his startled expression floated through Sophia's mind, followed by the memory of how that expression had turned appreciative a few seconds later.

"I'm so sorry," Phoebe said. "Ethan spoke to Ryder about the townhouse yesterday morning. We didn't know you'd arrive last night."

"It's okay." She waved a hand and shrugged. "No harm done. It's not like the guy hadn't seen me wearing less, all those years ago." As briefly as possible, she filled her friend in on her time with Ryder. "So, this morning was only mildly awkward. Besides, he didn't stick around long. After apologizing, he said he'd come back later, then left."

"Still, I feel awful. I'm sure that was not how you'd pictured running into him again."

"I hadn't pictured it at all," she fibbed...a little. "Kind of figured he was married with children by now."

Phoebe shook her head. "Nope. Single and unattached." Her friend grinned over her coffee. "In case you were wondering."

"No. I wasn't." Another fib.

The fact she had wondered didn't matter in the grand scheme of things. Digging out her laptop, she held onto that thought. "I can't wait to show you what I've come up with."

A subject change, but the Broadway star turned owner/producer didn't seem to mind.

"And I can't wait to see your designs." Phoebe rose to plop in a chair next to her and rubbed her hands together. "I'm so excited."

So was Sophia.

Helping to create memorable shows were just as important to her. It was her passion, too.

Work. Career. Leaving the family business. Those were the things she needed to concentrate on.

Not Ryder and his insanely good looks.

Or his wickedly talented mouth and hands.

Given that her attraction to the guy was still strong, she was definitely better off avoiding the sexy, *single, and unattached* guy.

Donna Michaels

Chapter Two

"Glad to see you could make it." Seated in their usual booth, Benjamin Wyne lifted his soda and grinned at Ryder.

He smirked. "Wiseass."

"I ordered you the usual, so if you want something different, you'll have to tell your dad."

"Thanks." He slid into the booth, across from his buddy and shook his head. "The usual's fine."

They'd been meeting at Gabe's—his father's restaurant—every Monday for lunch for several years now. Once in a while, he ordered something other than a burger and fries, but today was definitely a burger day. He needed to dig into something hearty to expel some of his pent-up aggravation.

Ben narrowed his eyes. "You lost another bid, didn't you?"

Muttering an oath, he scrubbed a hand over his face. "Colarusso snagged the Moleski account."

Renovating the local hardware store would've secured work for his second crew. Now, if he didn't land one, or both, of the two home renovation estimates he'd submitted last week, he might have to lay them off.

"Well, I have some news that might cheer you up," Ben said, regaining Ryder's attention.

"Oh? Are you and my sister having another baby?"

When he'd first found out his best friend was sleeping with his youngest sister, Ryder had been less than pleased. In fact, he'd punched Ben right in the face. After all, back then, his buddy had been way too popular with the ladies. But, Lea changed all that.

Married life and parenthood suited his friend. There was a contentment about him that had never been there before. Ben smiled easily, laughed often, and adoration and pride were evident in his eyes whenever he gazed at Lea and their month-old daughter.

"No." Smiling, Ben scratched the bridge of his nose. "Not that we don't want more kids, we do, but we agreed to wait until Melody is a year old before we start trying again."

Time to change the subject. Now that Ben was sleeping with his sister, talking sex was just wrong. And nauseating as hell.

"So." He sat back in his seat and eyed his buddy. "What news do you have that's supposed to cheer me up? You get your hands-on Mets tickets?"

Ben was full-time National Guard and in supply. He had a ton of contacts.

"This is better than Mets tickets." His buddy grinned, and the knowing look in his eyes made Ryder suddenly nervous. "Remember the friend from design school my sister brought home for New Year's Eve five years ago? Sophia? Well, she's back in town."

17

His pulse flickered at the mention of her name. "I know." He shrugged. "I ran into her this morning."

Ben's brows shot straight up. "No shit? Well, what happened? Are the sparks still there? Because, damn, man, the way the two of you hit it off that week was almost as crazy as the blue streaks in her hair. I mean, hell, you two disappeared for nearly two days. Poor Brandi hardly got to spend any time with her."

Guilt rippled through his gut. "There was too much wine and champagne flowing. We sort of lost track of time."

Ben snorted. "That's not all you lost, pal. As I recall, you mentioned something about the two of you'd spending most of that time naked in bed. Hell, you had a smile on your face for weeks."

Jesus…he'd told his buddy that? Then he'd definitely had too much to drink, because he never talked about being balls deep.

But Ben was right. He and Sophia had been naked most of the time, although the bed wasn't the only place they'd had sex. Incredible sex.

The memory had haunted him, because it had happened six months after he'd returned from Iraq without Jinan. It'd been so soon, and yet, Sophia had managed to make him forget the woman he'd loved. A blessing and a curse. One full of guilt.

"Here you go." The waitress arrived with their food and his iced tea.

"Hi, Elle," he said, reaching for two packets of sugar to sweeten his drink. "How's your first week of work going?"

"And the book?" Ben asked.

She was in town doing research on a police procedural romance, and when she wasn't going out on calls with their cop friend, Jeremy, she was here, helping his dad.

Smiling, she leaned against the booth and tipped her head. "As for the first question, things are going great here. Your dad is a sweetheart to work for, and I'm enjoying getting to meet so many locals. It's a big help with my research. As for the book...that's not going so great." She sighed. "Let's just say, Officer Mercer is not at all like your father to work with."

His chuckle echoed Ben's. "Yeah, Jeremy is a great cop, but outside of his job, he does tend to lack people skills."

She snickered. "Tell me about it. I sent him a link to an article on people etiquette, but he deleted it in front of me without even opening it."

Ben choked on his drink. "Did you really send him that link?"

"Yeah." She smiled. "Why?"

"Damn, I would've loved to have seen Jeremy's face." Ben grinned. "I hope you're going to bug him for a while."

Her chuckle mixed with his. "Yes, I'm not through with him...I mean, my research." She winked. "I still have a few weeks left, then I'm going to stick around your wonderful town while I write the book." She turned her gaze on him. "Thanks for letting me rent your cabin. It's perfect."

He thought so, too. "No problem."

Even though he now lived in a bigger one near the lake, he couldn't part with the single bedroom cabin. It'd been his first purchase and solo renovation when he was twenty. That was the reason he held onto it, not because of memories of an amazing New Year's Eve in the hot tub with a certain visiting city girl.

No, those memories, and the guilt of his enjoyment, were the reasons he'd moved out.

"Well, I'd better get back to work." She straightened. "More orders are up. Let me know if you two need anything else."

He nodded. "Will do."

Grinning, Ben cut into his open-faced meatloaf sandwich. "Man, I can't wait for drill this weekend."

"You're going to harass Jeremy, aren't you?" he asked, spreading mayo on his burger before adding ketchup to his fries.

"Damn straight." Ben nodded. "Too bad you didn't re-up when your contract ran out this spring. You could've joined in."

A smile tugged his lips. "Almost wish I had."

His buddy lifted a brow. "I can pull some strings and get you back in."

"No thanks," he said, lifting his burger. "I put in enough years. Besides, it's a young man's game. I'm nearing my mid-thirties."

"Hey, I'm the same age as you, pal."

He snickered. "Yeah, but you're full-time. It's your career. Mine is construction, and it's time I gave it my sole focus."

"You're right," Ben agreed. "But you sure are going to miss out on some fun this weekend. Unless you plan to invite Sophia to your bigger, better hot tub…"

Swallowing a curse, he eye-rolled his buddy. "You're an ass."

"Your sister happens to like my ass."

"Christ." He set his burger down in disgust. "What'd I tell you about that?"

The asshole laughed. "Sorry, can't resist. You make it so damn easy."

"Yeah, easy this." He flipped the idiot off, which only made him laugh harder.

Ethan walked in the door and immediately shook his head. "My brother's being his normal, annoying self, I see."

Ryder nodded as the oldest Wyne brother approached.

"He's family, I have to put up with him," Ethan teased. "You, on the other hand, can avoid the abuse, although, technically, he's your family too, since he's your brother-in-law."

He shrugged. "Guess I'm just unlucky and a masochist."

But in truth, Ben was a great friend. He'd had his back in battle, and on the home front. Hell, ever since kindergarten. His buddy had been there for him and his family when Ryder's mother had died in a car accident when he was eighteen. The poor guy had actually seen it in one of the visions he sometimes got. Ben had also been there for him when Jinan had chosen to fulfill a family duty and marry someone else.

No, Ben might be an idiot at times, but he was a solid friend.

"You have to be a masochist to put mayo on your burger." The guy's face wrinkled in disgust.

21

He dipped a fry in the leftover mayo, and holding Ben's gaze, he popped it into his mouth.

"Ah, seriously?" Gagging, his buddy pushed his half-eaten lunch aside. "Now who's being annoying?"

He turned to Ethan and grinned. "Care for some meatloaf?"

"Don't mind if I do."

Ryder moved over to make room for him, then laughed when Ben snatched his plate back.

"Not so fast. I can still eat while disgusted," his buddy claimed.

Ethan smirked. "Nothing comes between my brother and his food. Hell, you'll probably still eat when you're dead."

Ben nodded. "True."

Their laughter echoed through the restaurant, and Ryder was grateful to them for lightening his mood. No sense in letting Colarusso Construction ruin his lunch. They may have won the Moleski account, but he was determined they wouldn't win the next one.

"So…" Ben quirked a brow at his brother. "Were you present when Ryder was reunited with Sophia?"

Ethan's head snapped in his direction, disappointment creasing his brow. "No. I was unaware they'd seen each other again yet. Damn. I wanted to see it. Were the sparks still there?"

"I asked him the same thing, but he hasn't yet answered me," Ben said, gaze boring deep. "My guess is it's a big, fat yes, and he's in denial."

He reeled back. "Denial my ass."

"Yes, denial," Ben insisted. "Ever since Jinan, you've shut down, man. Frozen out any woman who tried to get close."

"It's true," Ethan said, snatching a fry from his plate.

Anger nipped at his shoulder blades. "Bullshit." He leaned forward and tapped the table with his finger. "Just because I'd rather focus on my business instead of women right now, doesn't mean I'm in denial." He sat back and smirked. "You're just butt-hurt because you didn't have a front row seat."

"Well, that's about to change," Ethan said. "Because Phoebe and Sophia are meeting me for lunch. And…look, here they are now."

Before he could respond or push the older Wyne idiot from the seat so he could get out, the door opened and in walked trouble.

Chapter Three

Trouble was right. Ryder's heart rocked in his chest. That was the first time it had moved for a woman in a long time.

Since Jinan. No…since Sophia.

She followed Phoebe inside, wearing a big smile on her face that outshined the sun and matched the yellow of her strapless sundress. Just like that, he remembered the silky feel of her supple skin and the taste of her sighs as he moved inside her.

Shit.

He stiffened and eyed the door. He needed to leave.

When he'd first walked in on her at Keiffer's that morning, he'd been in shock at finding the place occupied, and it hadn't worn off by the time he'd realized the woman he'd walked in on was Sophia.

But now, the shock was gone, and as she approached the table and her gaze found his, waves of awareness began to blast his body. It was like thawing out in front of a fire after coming in from a snow storm.

Dammit.

His buddy had gotten it wrong. It wasn't women he froze out, it was his heart, or at least what was left of the battered organ in his chest.

"Phoebe. Sophia," the Wyne brothers said in unison, as they shot to their feet.

Ryder followed suit, and as much as he longed to escape out the door, the good manners his mother had managed to instill in him kept him from fleeing. But when they moved to a big table, and he found himself seated across from *trouble*, he was sorry he hadn't bolted when he'd had the chance.

Elle came over and took the newcomer's orders, giving him a chance to regroup.

"She's in town doing research for a book," Ben informed the women.

Phoebe's face lit up. "You're an author?"

"Yes, I write romance novels."

Sophia sat up. "I love them. What's your pen name?"

"Elena Pratt."

Phoebe sucked in a breath. "Oh my God."

"No way." Sophia smiled. "That's freaking awesome. I have all your books."

"So do I, and Lea and Jill do, too." Phoebe pointed to Ben.

His buddy squirmed and held up his hands. "I don't have any of your books."

Phoebe laughed. "I was going to tell Elena that Lea is your wife, and Jill is my sister-in-law."

"Please, call me Elle. And thank you." A blush rose into her cheeks. "I'm so glad you like my work."

"We love your work." Phoebe smiled. "You have to come to our weekly Thursday night chocolate fest." She turned to Sophia. "You, too."

"You had me at chocolate fest." Sophia chuckled, and the sound did strange things to Ryder's chest.

Refocusing on his food, he tried to ignore the odd current emanating from the woman. How the hell could he feel that? They weren't even touching.

Christ. He was acting like a damn teenager.

"Thank you," Elle said. "I'd love to come. No way would I pass up the opportunity to pick your brains." She winked. "Besides, you said the magic word—chocolate. It's an author's necessity. Well, one of two. Coffee is the other. We mainline that sucker." She pulled her phone from her apron pocket. "Just tell me where and what time?"

Phoebe rocked in her seat. "That's great. We meet at the Confection Connection right down the block, just after it closes. Jill's the owner. She and her husband are in California on business, but she left me her keys. She didn't want us to cancel our get-togethers."

"Remind me to thank her," Sophia said.

"Me, too." Elle nodded, holding up her pad. "I'll go put in your orders and come back with your drinks."

As she left, he reached for his iced tea, happy to stay out of the conversation.

"Sophia." Ben frowned at her. "What's up with your eyes?"

Ethan nodded. "Yeah. Didn't you have one brown and one blue?"

A small smile tugged her lips. "Still do, underneath brown contacts."

"You do?" Phoebe asked. "I never knew that. I bet they're amazing."

"They are," he said, without realizing it...until everyone stopped to stare at him. He shrugged and refocused on his food.

"I just prefer to see the same color when I look in the mirror," she said.

"Nothing wrong with that," Phoebe proclaimed, and he silently agreed.

Growing up, kids had probably done a number on her. He knew how cruel they could be. He'd found out the hard way, after his mother's death.

"So, Sophia," Ben began, and Ryder stiffened at the teasing tone, knowing he was not going to like the next words to come out of his friend's mouth. "My buddy, here, was just about to tell us where the two of you bumped into each other this morning. Care to enlighten us?"

Color rising into her cheeks, she met his gaze and smiled. Unwanted warmth spread through his chest.

"We met in Keiffer's bedroom."

Ah, hell. Here we go.

Ben's attention snapped to him. "That's probably why he didn't tell me."

"I'd just gotten out of the shower and walked into the bedroom a second before he entered," she continued, still holding his gaze.

Ryder's heart rocked against his ribs, because her confession was the last thing his buddy needed to hear. It had nothing to do with the memory of her mile-long legs and the wet towel clinging to her lush curves.

The woman had been sexy as hell before…now she was fucking hot.

And he had a hard-on to prove it. Second one that day, thanks to her.

Son-of-a-bitch.

He shifted in his seat to relieve the pressure from his zipper, and bided his time to leave.

"That's definitely why he didn't tell me."

Ben's chuckle drifted over him, and it affectively helped to cool his stupid libido.

"I'm really sorry," Ethan said. "I was the one who asked him to fix a few things before you arrived. I hadn't realized you were already there."

She leaned forward to glance around Phoebe, at Ethan. "It's all right. And all my fault. Phoebe told me the key was at the desk, so I drove in late last night. I couldn't wait to get out of the city."

Surprise rippled through him. He thought she loved the city.

"It's a good thing you knew Ryder, then," Ben said, smile twitching his lips.

Jackass.

He refrained from elbowing the bastard. Barely. "I'm sure I startled you all the same," he said. "I'm sorry."

"There's no need to apologize." She smiled that thousand-watt smile again, and all sorts of needs rushed through him.

Dammit.

Latching onto the need to flee, he rose to his feet. "I have to get back to work." He tossed money on the table to cover his food and tip. "Catch you guys later."

Nodding to them, he noted disappointment flashed through her eyes, and a knowing smirk spread across his buddy's face.

Yeah, definitely time to cut and run.

Over the last few years, he'd worked hard to try to leave the past behind, and Sophia was technically part of his past. Last thing he needed was to revisit something that could topple his house of cards. Even if she wasn't the one who'd hurt him.

But given his crazy reactions to her today, he recognized she had the ability to get to him.

That wasn't gonna happen.

Chapter Four

That afternoon, Sophia walked with Phoebe toward the theater, enjoying the soft breeze blowing off the lake. They'd both agreed it was much too nice outside to drive over, so they took the scenic route behind the resort.

The Wyne brothers had pooled their money and bought the place, then hired their sister to revamp it into a year-round resort. She stopped to turn around and admire her college friend's handiwork. Nestled between trees, the resort blended with the surroundings, thanks to its wooden exterior, and the floor to ceiling windows in some of the areas brought nature inside.

"This place is amazing," she said. "Before she left for Texas, Brandi had been urging me to visit, but I was always too busy with work and couldn't get the time off."

Phoebe nodded. "I understand. I was married to my work for years. But I started to get restless, then I met Ethan and his son Tyler, and, well, everything fell into place. My life changed for the better. I've slowed down, reprioritized, and I've never been so happy."

"I can tell." She smiled. "You have a glow about you."

Her friend blushed. "It's not just Ethan and Tyler, it's the fact I'm about to give back to help the youth in this area. There's so much talent, it's amazing. And it's also sad. These kids didn't have anywhere to showcase their talent, or the opportunity to grow."

"Well, they do now, thanks to you," she said, as they continued to walk toward a big building she spied in the distance. "And I was wondering if any are interested in set design? Or if there's a local technical school or college where I can hire some helpers?"

Phoebe's smile widened. "That's a wonderful idea. Ryder's already volunteered to help out with the sets, and he actually already mentors a few carpentry students from the local college. I bet he could hook you up."

Her heart rocked at the mention of Ryder and hookup. Been there, done that. Enjoyed it. Too much.

She needed to get a grip.

That wasn't why she was in town. Besides, he was in construction, and despite how sexy he looked sporting a tool belt, she was surrounded by men in tool belts all day. Every day.

Her entire life.

Meeting a guy in a different profession would be a breath of fresh air. But none of that mattered, because judging by his abrupt exit at lunch, she got the impression the last thing he wanted to do was hookup with her again.

Although, considering the bomb Phoebe just dropped, avoiding each other was going to be difficult if they were working together.

She cleared her suddenly dry throat. "I'll ask him."

Hopefully, he wouldn't have a problem with her taking the lead. It was her design and she had no intention of letting someone else run with it, no matter how damn cute he was.

"I have to admit, I found it interesting that he left lunch so abruptly today." Phoebe scratched her temple and grinned. "He's usually calm and cool. So, yeah, I found that very interesting. My guess is you're a blast from his past that sent a tremor in the force."

Forcing a smile, she sighed. "Ethan told you more than I thought."

Phoebe nodded. "He said you two instantly hit it off over a holiday weekend several years ago."

"It was just a brief thing." She shrugged. "No biggie."

"Well, I hope you're okay to work with him. I feel bad for already lining him up to help."

She set a hand on her friend's shoulder. "It's fine. Please don't worry about it."

"Super. So…let's change the subject. What do you think of the place?" Phoebe asked as they neared.

"Wow." She stopped to take in the structure that was a lot taller and grander than she'd first realized. And made of reinforced concrete. "You went art deco. I love it."

Her friend grinned. "Me, too. It's what I wanted. The more Streamline Modern version from the

1930's. Brandi designed everything I'd asked for, and Ryder delivered it down to the very last detail." She nodded toward a cluster of cars in the parking lot. "Good. My assistant is already here, which means the doors are unlocked and the lights are already on. Wait until you see the inside."

Bold geometric designs, chevrons, and zigzags met Sophia's gaze as she stepped into the past. A glamorous one. "Reminds me of the Chrysler Building, and one of the art deco theaters in Oakland."

"Exactly." Phoebe beamed.

Black marble covered the walls halfway up, with gold horizontal stripes running the length of the walls. The rest of the walls were a series of tall, tan arches, with a gold, lit panel and a decorative rail inside the arches.

Straight ahead was a U-shaped stairway with risers on each side that met in an arch shape to form a balcony on the second floor.

"I originally wanted a marbled staircase, but it felt safer to go with the same carpet as the lobby. So, we decided on a decorative black wrought iron rail to match the walls."

"It's perfect." She smiled, then rushed up the stairs to gaze out over the lobby. "Truly perfect."

Laughing, Phoebe met her upstairs. "I think so, too. Come on, you have to see the main theater." The enthusiastic artist tugged her into the balcony of a grand theater with décor of gold and black, but also cream and red.

"I bet the acoustics are amazing," she said, eyeing up the high ceiling with more geometric designs and art deco lighting.

Phoebe nodded. "I consulted a specialist. That was the most important detail. Come on." She grabbed Sophia's hand again. "Let me show you the rest."

On the left of the main stage was a hall that led to a smaller theater, and two soundproof classrooms where a few students were already starting to gather. After a few quick introductions, she followed Phoebe to the right of the main stage, into a large wardrobe room complete with racks for costumes, tables, sewing machines, and a long shelf holding reams of fabric.

"Holy smokes." She blinked. "It's like a mini factory."

Phoebe chuckled. "I wanted to make sure wardrobe has everything that's needed. There are still a few shipments that haven't come in yet." Her smile widened as she led her to the final door. "I saved the best for last."

Some of her friend's excitement wore off on her, upping her pulse as the door opened to the room of her dreams.

"Oh. My. God." Goose bumps covered her skin. "I'm in heaven." Shelves stocked with paints and tools and material lined the far wall, and alongside were several stacks of plywood and a utility sink. She blinked, walking further into an actual space designated for set design. "Set design heaven."

Her friend chuckled. "Ryder did a fantastic job."

Right. She'd forgotten. The man was the one responsible for the whole incredible building. "He sure did. It's perfect. I think I'll move my bed in here and never leave."

"Good." Phoebe winked. "I was hoping you'd say that, because I'd love to work with you permanently here."

She reeled back. "You would?"

"Absolutely." Her friend nodded. "I know it's not Broadway, but this place…it's special. I can feel it."

So did Sophia. She still had the goose bumps to prove it. But her dream to design a Broadway set hadn't happened yet. Sure, she'd worked on them, but was never hired as the sole designer. Her goal. Her dream.

"I'm truly flattered, and definitely tempted," she finally said.

"But, you have your heart set on Broadway." Phoebe smiled. "It's okay. I get it. Believe me."

She nodded. "I got a callback for the Rodgers and Hammerstein musical."

Her friend's eyes widened. "South Pacific?"

She nodded again. It was her all-time favorite of their musicals.

A shrieking Phoebe rushed over to pull her in for a hug. "Oh my God, Sophia! That's terrific! And you're just telling me now? When is your callback?"

"Mid-September," she replied, drawing back.

"I'm thrilled for you. If there's anything I can do to help, just let me know."

Warmed by the generous offer, she smiled. "Thanks. I will. But right now, I'm excited to nail down the designs for *your* Rodgers and Hammerstein production."

Oklahoma was another of her favorites.

"I think you pretty much have."

She patted her purse. "If you don't mind, I'm going to sit in the main theater and double-check my sight lines." A set was useless if there were patrons unable to see it. "Then I'd like to fill in a few of my sketches."

"Go right ahead." Phoebe glanced at the time on her phone. "I've got that class to teach. Most of the students were already there when we dropped in during the tour."

She nodded, and after one last glance at the magical room, she headed into the main theater. The collaboration between Phoebe and Brandi resulted in a one-of-a-kind performing arts building, but it was Ryder who brought it all to life. Spectacularly.

No matter which section she sat in to check her sight lines, Sophia marveled at the talented carpenter's execution. Art Deco wasn't exactly a practiced style these days, especially in the middle of the woods, and yet, Ryder nailed it, with a capital N.

Admiration upped her pulse. That was two things the man was good at. She wasn't sure she could handle a third.

***

By the time Ryder doubled back to Keiffer's place and fixed the drain in the master bathroom, the sun was starting to set. Shit. He gathered his tools, and hurried across the room. The last thing he needed was to run into Sophia again.

It was bad enough he was going to have to work with her at the theater. If he had known she was the set designer Phoebe gushed about, he would've...what? Refused to help? No way. Volunteering to work on a set was the perfect hands-on lessons for the two college kids he mentored.

Still...why did it have to be Sophia?

As if fate were laughing at him, the woman in question walked into the room.

"Hi, Ryder," she said, not in the least bit startled this time. "It's kind of a reverse déjà vu."

He, on the other hand, needed a moment to steady his pulse. Damn thing. "Hey, Sophia. I just finished up in the bathroom. You shouldn't have any more issues with the sink."

Jesus, he was babbling like a high schooler. And why was she sitting down on the bed?

"Okay, great. I...uh...didn't know there was a problem." She slipped a finger beneath the strap around her ankle and removed her sandal. "I hope I didn't create a mess."

"No. Not at all," he said, gripping his toolbox tightly, as she repeated the process on the other foot. "I don't think you used it. The one on the right just needed a washer."

"Ah...I've been using the left sink." She stood up and smiled. "And you've been busy creating a masterpiece."

He raised a brow. "I have?"

"Yes." Admiration lit her eyes, and son-of-a-bitch, his heart cracked open a little. "I spent the afternoon at the theater, and it didn't take long to realize you aren't just a carpenter, Ryder. You're a craftsman."

His chest swelled at her unexpected compliment. "Thank you." Not many people knew the difference.

But, this was Sophia, and even though her eyes were one color, and hair was a traditional color now, she wasn't most people.

"Between the theater and what I've seen of this resort, I just wanted you to know I think your work is amazing," she said. "And I look forward to working with you on the sets."

More compliments.

Growing increasingly uncomfortable, he shifted the weight on his feet. If it weren't for the flash of surprise in her eyes at her admission, he'd think she was fishing for a compliment in return.

She wasn't getting one. He couldn't tell her he looked forward to working with her too...because he didn't. The woman was trouble. And unlike a certain New Year's Eve many years ago, he wasn't looking for any.

"I have a few more things to take care of at the resort, so I should get going," he said. "If you find anything else wrong with the place, let Ethan know."

By rights, he could've told her to let him know, but he needed to keep her at arm's length. To keep things professional.

Her smile faltered. "Okay. Sure."

Now, he felt like a dick, because he was one. But it wasn't just for his own good. It was for hers, too.

Other than work, she didn't need him in her life. He let people down.

He wasn't worth it.

"Have a good evening," he said on his way out the door.

The sooner he left, the better. His chest was already growing heavy with guilt. He didn't need that crap. He needed to focus on work. Starting with the mound of paperwork on his desk back at the office.

Twenty-five minutes later, Ryder wished he'd just gone home. The pile had taken over the top of his desk.

"Do you want me to order some pizza from Martelli's?" Cathy, his assistant leaned against his doorway, pity darkening her eyes.

He sat back in his chair and nodded. "Yeah. Thanks. Looks like I'm going to be here longer than I thought."

She nodded and made to turn away.

"Any news on those bids?"

"No." She turned around to face him again. "No word yet. And I'm sorry about the Moleski project."

He blew out a breath. "Yeah. Me, too."

He was sorry about a lot of things. Sorry he was struggling to find work for his men. Sorry he hadn't gone to the store when his mother had asked the day she'd died. Sorry he was unable to stop the woman he loved from marrying a stranger her parents had arranged. Sorry he put the hurt in Sophia's eyes when she was being generous with a compliment.

She'd called him a craftsman.

A smile tugged his lips while unexpected warmth seeped into his chest. That was sweet of her. She seemed less rebellious, subdued even. But still sexy as hell. An image of her—wrapped in that damn towel—flashed through his mind. His dick twitched.

39

Son-of-a-bitch.

First, she caused movement in his chest, now below his belt.

He was sorry he had to be rude to her, but not sorry he *was* rude. It was necessary, thanks to the crazy attraction still sizzling between them. With him scheduled to work with the set designer—her—throughout the summer, physical distance wasn't an option. However, the same wasn't true for emotional distance.

Hopefully, she'd gotten the message and wouldn't waste her time on him, because there was no way he could fight their chemistry for even a week, let alone several months.

Ryder needed to create an invisible wall between them, and counted on his rudeness to lay the foundation for that barrier.

He glanced at his wall calendar.

Time would tell soon—real soon—if it worked.

Two days from now, he was scheduled to meet her at the theater to discuss the project and timeline. With luck, Sophia would treat him with indifference. If not, he'd have no choice but to up the surly factor.

Chapter Five

After spending a day and a half on renderings to include the scene changes Phoebe had added, Sophia worked on ground plans—a bird's eye view—for each scene. This gave her a good base to start her three-dimensional models for each set.

Using the amazing set design room and all its resources, she managed to complete three and a half before Phoebe arrived ten minutes early for their meeting with Ryder.

"Oh my God, Sophia, these are amazing." Clapping her hands, the woman practically vibrated as she walked from model to model placed on the table where Sophia was finishing up the final one.

She smiled. "Thanks. I've never been able to build them so fast before. I'm seriously in love with this room."

"The whole building is amazing." Phoebe grinned. "I'm blessed."

"How'd rehearsal go?" she asked, rummaging through a bin of doll furniture, looking for a rocking chair and hay bale.

She found both. Perfect.

Phoebe cleared her throat. "That's actually why I'm here."

Carrying them back to the table, she eyed her friend. "Something wrong?"

"No. Actually, it's going good," Phoebe replied. "The cast wants to stay and rehearse a little longer. But I wanted to stop in first and see what you've come up with, and also to ask if you'd mind coordinating the schedule with Ryder? He's going to basically be working with you, anyhow."

Sophia's pulse hiccupped like it always did whenever someone mentioned the guy's name. "Of course. No problem." She grabbed the glue and proceeded to affix the rocking chair to the model, holding it in place a few seconds so it would stick.

Now, if she could just get her stupid body under control before the man arrived, that'd be great. She glued the hay bale to the model, and held it in place.

"Thanks. I appreciate it," Phoebe said. "I'd better get back. See ya later." With a quick nod, her friend turned and rushed out of the room.

Given Ryder's track record, he was liable to do the same thing when he discovered they were on their own tonight.

Not her problem.

She released the bale, then stood back to view the finished product, but the model came with her. The bale was stuck to the model and her hand.

"Wow, you really take three-dimensional to a whole new depth," Ryder said, walking toward her with a grin.

The instant fluttering in her belly momentarily distracted her from the fact she wore her model as a glove. Shaking the fog from her head, she set the model back on the table and returned his grin. "Always looking for a way to stand out."

He frowned. "I thought you didn't like to stand out."

"As a person, no, but as a set designer, yes. Standing out is good." It was a necessity, in order to succeed. And she needed her hand in order to work. She was such an idiot.

"Ah." He came up behind her and reached for her hand. "Let me help."

Even if she'd wanted to tell him no—which she didn't—it was impossible. The feel of his solid chest brushing her back dried her throat. Damn, he smelled great. Like soap and cedar, with a hint of some kind of spice.

Warm fingers covered hers, and the scrape of calluses on her skin sent a ripple of awareness straight up her arm. Where was his wall of indifference now? It usually sprang up between them before they ever got this close.

"Just relax. Let me do all the work."

Her mind immediately went to a naughty place, and she had to fight hard to suppress the tremors that threatened.

Back and forth, he gently tugged, until her hand was free. By that time, awareness spread to every blood vessel in her body, and every inch of her was aware of the change in his breathing.

And the fact he still held her hand.

She turned her head slightly to see his face. Heaven help her, his eyes had darkened to a stormy blue. Her heart rocked in her chest, disrupting her hold on those tremors.

His jaw clenched, and a second later, he abruptly released her and stepped back. "You might want to wash the glue off your hand."

Unable to switch from aroused to indifferent as quickly as Ryder, she nodded and headed to the utility sink across the room. With distance between them, she regained control and the ability to breathe normally again.

That was batshit crazy.

As she washed and dried her hands, she pondered how to break it to the guy that they were on their own tonight. But since he was the one with the problem, and not her, she decided to treat it like it was no big deal. They were two adults working on a project. Turning around, she cleared her throat and walked back to her models, careful to keep the table between them, because...dammit, her body was still tingling. "Phoebe's not coming."

His brows furrowed and panic briefly skittered through his eyes. But he didn't take flight. "Is she all right?"

"Yes." She nodded. "They're rehearsing longer tonight. But, I already have her schedule. It's on the wall there by the door. So you and I can come up with a game plan that fits into your schedule. I'm easy. I mean, flexible. Wide open." Dammit. Heat rushed into her face. "What I'm trying to say is I'm available...I can come anytime. Seriously? Just kill me now." She slapped a hand over mouth and shook her head, noting a smile tugging his lips.

"Hey, are you Sophia and Ryder?" A teenager walked in, carrying a box of pizza and two bottles of water. "Phoebe told me to bring this to you."

Her friend must've ordered supper for the troops.

"Yes. Thanks," she said, and the boy set everything on the table by her, then left. "Well that was perfect timing." She turned to Ryder and grinned. "I was getting tired of the taste of my foot. I'd much rather shove a piece of pizza in my mouth."

Chuckling, he grabbed two folded chairs stacked against the wall and carried them over. "I thought it was cute."

For the first time since she'd returned, he visibly relaxed. His shoulders and mouth were no longer stiff, and she was happy to adopt his friendly attitude. One should never underestimate the power of pizza.

Over the next hour, they shared dinner and a few more laughs while hammering out a schedule that worked around his job. It didn't take long for her to remember what had drawn her to the guy all those years ago—his wit and intelligence. Yeah, he was also gorgeous, but she'd grown up around handsome guys her whole life. In her world, they were plentiful. Ryder stood out. He was...more. And like his good looks, his wit and intelligence had also matured and increased.

"These are amazing, Sophia." He nodded to the sketches, plans, and models spread out on the table. "You're very good."

His compliments sent a wave of warmth through her chest. He had a way of making her feel alive. Vibrant. No one else had ever made her feel so good about herself.

"Thanks." She wiped her hands off on her jeans, and stood. "I still have to work on elevations of each set."

Rising to his feet, he frowned. "Scaled sketches?"

"Exactly. Once I finish those, then I can write down building instructions. There not just for you, though, they're for everyone," she rushed to explain.

He nodded, no signs of offense in his eyes. "I would imagine you need to use lightweight material, so the sets are easy to move."

"Yes. For the flats—backgrounds—we frame out paintable material like muslin." She grabbed a pencil and paper and sketched out a quick diagram of a flat. After answering his questions about materials, she went on to briefly explain the construction of platforms and collapsible platforms, called parallels.

He tapped the paper with his finger and smiled. "These will be great for the kids to construct."

"The college kids Phoebe mentioned?"

"Yeah, I have a few interning with me over the summer," he said. "Wish I could pay them, but at least they're getting experience."

She nodded. "That's how I started out in set design." She'd worked for her father during the day, then spent hours at night volunteering her time and expertise at several theaters. "I was thrilled at the chance. Speaking of which, do you think you could find a few more who'd be interested in helping out?"

He straightened and faced her, surprise lifting his brows. "Yeah. I'm sure the college has several that'd be interested."

"Perfect." She smiled. "How about art students? I'd love to give a few locals the chance to tap into their skills and creativity, and help with the four backgrounds required in this production."

"You'd do that?"

"Absolutely." She grinned at the incredulity in his tone. "I'm so grateful for the opportunities I was given. And now, I'm excited to be in the position to pay it forward."

An unrecognizable emotion flickered through his eyes, before a pleased expression settled in those mesmerizing blue depths. "That's really great, Sophia. I'll stop by the college this Friday."

"Can I go with you?" she asked. "I'd like to talk to the art teacher."

He nodded. "Of course. I'll swing by here around ten to pick you up. Or will you be at the townhouse?"

"I'll be here. Thanks. I appreciate you hooking me up."

As soon as she said it, his gaze darkened, then dropped to her lips. Damn...that was the look that always revved her engines. All her good parts instantly sparked to life, and a shiver of heat rippled down to her toes.

She didn't remember their attraction being this strong.

His smile slowly faded about the same time her heart rocked hard in her chest. They stood there, barely a foot apart, staring at each other. She didn't dare to breathe, or blink. But she knew she needed to move. Trouble was, she couldn't remember if moving away, or stepping closer was the right thing to do.

His gaze was a stormy blue, no doubt reflecting his inner turmoil. She wanted to make him feel better, but the line between what she wanted and what *he* needed began to blur.

A second later they lunged for each other.

His hands were in her hair, holding her still while his mouth devoured hers in a kiss that was as demanding as it was giving. Deep, hungry, scintillatingly thorough, he proceeded to wipe every single thought from her mind, except one. More. She needed more.

Cupping the back of his head, she brushed her tongue against his, remembering the exact stroke that used to drive him mad. A low, sexy sound rumbled deep in his chest, and one of his wonderful hands ran down her back to cup her ass and crush her closer.

Another sexy sound emanated between them. This time it came from her. He had her vibrating with need, made her want things. Everything.

God, she'd missed this heady rush…this out-of-control feeling.

When he stiffened and suddenly released her, she blinked and grasped the table behind her for balance. "What's wrong? Why'd you stop?"

Chapter Six

With a mirthless laugh, Ryder shook his head. "Because it should've never started. I'm sorry, Sophia. That was my fault." He made to walk away, but she grabbed his arm.

"The hell it was." Her chin rose, and eyes flashed with indignation. "I was a fully participating...*participant* in that kiss, too, Ryder."

Damn, she was beautiful, and that kiss just proved their explosive chemistry had nothing to do with wine or champagne all those years ago. Her gaze was locked on his mouth, and he could tell she wanted his on hers again.

Bad idea.

A piece of her long hair stuck to his stubbled jaw. He reached up to brush it away, but ended up wrapping the silky strand around his finger instead.

Christ, he had no fucking clue what he was doing.

That explained why he kissed her again. Another wild, off-the-hinges, tongues tangling, rock-his-world kiss that left him reeling when they broke apart for air. She leaned against the table, breathing ragged, gaze as dazed as he felt. Working to catch his breath, he stared at her lips, still wet from his kisses, and barely managed to refrain from pulling her in a third time.

What the hell was wrong with him?

He drew in a deeper breath, then another, waiting for the axis to tip back and right his stupid world.

Never fucking happened.

Not good.

It was time to go. "That can't happen again."

Her gaze narrowed. "Why not?"

Jesus, now was not the time for her old rebellious nature to kick in. He straightened his spine. "You need to steer clear of me, Sophia."

"Kind of hard to do when we're going to be working together." Her tone was full of the same derision gleaming in her eyes.

Muffling a curse, he scrubbed a hand over his face and stared hard at her. "You know what I mean."

"No, I don't." That damn brow lifted again. "Enlighten me."

Hell, no. No way was he about to discuss their crazy-ass kisses, and the fact his whole world tilted.

"You're a smart girl. You'll figure it out," he said, then twisted around and strode out the door.

***

Sophia screwed the last screw in place, then set the drill down before stepping back to view the corkboard she'd just added to the wall. Perfect. She ordered a whiteboard as well, but it hadn't arrived yet. For now, though, she was at least able to hang the corkboard, so she had a place to pin a copy of her final sketches.

She'd spent the last two days immersed in work, determined to finish all her sketches to scale, as well as the directions to build each set. After pinning a copy of each set design to the corkboard, she put away her drill. Tomorrow morning, she was heading to the college with Ryder. If the professors needed to see the designs to determine if the project was worthwhile, she'd have another copy of them in hand to help ensure the students would get credits for their course.

Working on them the past two days had also served another purpose. It kept her mind off Ryder and his crazy, hot kisses. The ones that knocked her socks off—or would have if she hadn't been wearing sandals—before he flicked the indifference switch and walked away. Again.

He really needed to stop doing that.

"Hey, Sophia, are you ready for some wine and chocolate?" Phoebe waltzed into the set room, with a big grin on her face. "It's Thursday night—time for the weekly chocolate fest."

Oh, hell yeah. She pushed the chair under the table she'd used earlier, and nodded. "Am I ever."

Phoebe's chuckle echoed around the room. "I can see I don't have to ask you twice."

"Not at all." She grabbed her purse and was at her friend's side in a heartbeat. "I need chocolate. Bad. In all forms. Now."

"Then allow me to take you to paradise." Phoebe wiggled her keys, and together they locked up the building, before getting in her friend's car and heading to town. "Lea has the key and is meeting us there. She's excited to see you again. And to meet Elle."

Lea was fun and smart, and Brandi's best friend. The three of them had hung out several times over the years. "I can't wait to see her again, too. She texted me a few hours ago, during her train ride back from the city."

"Yeah," Phoebe said, driving down the country road that led to Main Street. "I think she's technically still on maternity leave, but had to go in a few days because of a new exhibit."

Sophie laughed, recalling the conversation. "She said something about sleeping with her baby girl this afternoon, then possibly her husband, before meeting us to refuel on chocolate."

"Sounds like Lea." Snickering, Phoebe parked in front of a quaint little shop that had a brown awning, with light blue stripes. "Looks like she's already inside with Elle."

Getting out of the car, Sophia stepped onto the sidewalk and was too busy admiring the architecture of the building to notice the man exiting the shop. She walked right into a brick wall of warmth that smelled of soap and cedar and some kind of spice.

Ryder.

"Sorry." He gripped her arms and used his body to steady her. "Are you okay?"

Heat flooded her belly and funneled south.

Define okay.

"Yeah," she managed. But, she would've been even better if he laid one of his mind-blowing kisses on her.

Shoot. Thoughts like that were going to get her in trouble.

He stiffened—no doubt because he recognized her—and as usual, his indifference did little to lessen her attraction to the man. It was maddening.

Doing her best to ignore the urge to rub against him like a cat, she squashed down the hysterical laughter bubbling up her throat, and pushed free of his hold. Phoebe and the two women inside the shop were way too interested in their collision.

"Sorry. It was my fault," she said, meeting his gaze. "I was admiring the building and failed to watch where I was going."

Something unreadable flickered through his eyes.

Then it dawned on her. "You built this, too, didn't you?"

He shrugged, looking a bit uncomfortable. "A few years ago."

Shaking her head, she smiled. "Well, it's amazing. I really do love your attention to detail." And she knew firsthand that attention spilled over into his sex life. Her damn knees wobbled at the memory. "Are we still on for tomorrow morning?"

He blinked, as if trying to clear his brain, and she wondered if perhaps some memories from their night together had passed through his mind, too.

"Ah…yeah." He nodded. "Ten o'clock."

"Perfect," she said, and with a nod, she left him on the sidewalk and entered the building, determined to be the one to walk away this time. Once inside, she smiled at the two women staring at her with interest. "Hi, Elle. Lea."

The latter greeted her with a hug. "It's great to see you again, Sophia."

"You, too." She drew back and raised a brow. "When do I get to see that little girl of yours?"

Happiness flushed the new mother's face. "How's tomorrow? I plan to stop by the theater."

"Better make it before ten," Phoebe said, coming up behind them. "She's got a date with Ryder at ten."

Lea sucked in a breath. "You do? That's wonderful. I was hoping you two would hit it off again."

She shook her head. "It's not a date-date."

"Damn. That's too bad." Lea frowned. "My brother is single, disillusioned, and grumpy."

For a moment, she'd forgotten Ryder was her brother.

"Sounds like another guy I know in town," Elle said, with an eye roll. "Although, having met them both, Officer Mercer is definitely worse."

Even though she'd never met Officer Mercer, Sophia joined in the laughter while they all took their seats at a table already loaded with slices of thick chocolate cake.

Her stomach growled.

Yeah, it was time to feed the monster.

She slid a plate closer, picked up a fork, then dug in. Her palate immediately rejoiced. Moist and rich, the cake melted in her mouth, and the deep, rich chocolate taste was to die for. Her moan echoed the others in a joyous melody.

"So, who is Officer Mercer, and how do you know him?" she asked Elle after devouring half her slice. "Did he pull you over for speeding or something?"

"No," the author snickered. "I'm researching a police procedural. He's letting me ride along with him for research." She held up a hand. "Let me rephrase that. He's being *forced to chauffer a bodice-ripper novelist around instead of doing his job.* Those are his words."

Sophia and the others laughed. "You don't write bodice rippers. You don't even write historicals. And your books are deep, and layered, and the sex enhances the story."

"I don't think he reads anything but newspapers," Elle scoffed.

Lea smiled. "Man, this is awesome. I wish I could see his face as he's forced to drive you around. Don't get me wrong, Jeremy is a great guy, but he does take his job seriously. This assignment would definitely disrupt his orderly routine."

"Well, too bad, so sad for him." Elle shrugged. "It's not like I'm keeping him from doing his job, despite what he claims. I'm just there to observe, so I get it all correct in my book. It's better than letting me misrepresent him."

"Exactly." Phoebe nodded. "I had to ride along with the L.A.P.D. when I was researching my movie role last winter. It was amazing, and scary, to see what their daily lives entail. And it was important to me to portray the police force correctly."

"I told Officer Mercer the same thing," Elle said. "But he still grumbles."

"That's because he has a penis," Lea said, matter-of-factly, scooping cake onto her fork.

Sophia and the others chuckled. The woman was hysterical.

"It's true." Lea shrugged. "And the more alpha they are, the more they grumble."

"Then Officer Mercer is as alpha as they get," Elle said, distaste twisting her lips.

"Seems to me he's kind of getting to you," she said. "Does he happen to be handsome?"

Color increased in the author's face as she shrugged. "If you go for the blue-eyed, muscular type of guy."

Considering Ryder had blue eyes and a nice array of muscles, Sophia figured she was guilty. It was best to keep her mouth shut.

"So, Sophia...if it's not a date-date, then what exactly are you doing with my brother tomorrow morning?" Lea asked, curiosity sparking in eyes the same blue shade as Ryder's.

"It's a work thing," she replied, frustrated to have the subject resurrected. "He's taking me to the local college, so I can see about getting some students to help with the sets."

"Do your bodies know it's not a date-date?" Elle asked, lazy smile on her lips. "I'm a people watcher. It's great research for my books. So I'm pretty good at reading people, and, well, your bodies were definitely speaking an intimate language."

"It's because they have a history," Lea said.

Interest sparked in the author's eyes. "Oh, really?"

Phoebe nodded. "I believe it was a New Year's Eve, several years ago."

Elle pushed an auburn strand of hair behind her ear, and cocked her head. "No, what I was reading was something a lot more recent."

All three women stared at her now. Great.

She sighed. "What?"

"You tell us?" Lea narrowed her gaze. "Did something happen recently?"

"And did it have anything to do with his weird departure from the restaurant the other day?" Elle asked.

Phoebe reeled back. "You saw that too?"

"Yep." The redhead winked. "People watcher."

"Well? Go on...tell me, what did you see? I wasn't there." Lea huffed.

Stuffing more cake in her mouth, Sophia continued to eat while the others filled the anxious woman in on her brother's strange behavior."

"He's definitely still feeling you." Lea grinned. "I was beginning to think he'd never feel anything for a woman again."

Her heart squeezed. "What do you mean?"

A deep sigh filled the air. "Several months before that New Year's Eve, Ryder came home from deployment a different man. A broken one," Lea added, sadness deepening her tone.

"Did he lose someone over there?" Elle's question echoed the one in Sophia's mind.

Lea nodded. "I believe so. But, it wasn't anyone from his unit. They all came back, thank God."

"What made you think Ryder suffered a loss?" she asked, her chest tight at the thought of him going through that type of pain.

"He returned home with the same dark, devastated, guilt ridden look in his eyes that he'd had after our mother died," Lea replied. "I asked him what happened, but he just shook his head and said he didn't want to talk about it."

The tightness in Sophia's chest increased. She'd felt that way when her Nona had passed.

"I don't know. I think it had something to do with a woman. But six months later, you came in with Brandi for the holiday, and bam." Smiling, Lea slapped the table. "There was life behind his eyes again. Although, the past few years it's been gone."

"Not anymore." Phoebe winked. "There's definitely a spark."

Elle pointed her fork at her. "Like I said, something has happened recently."

"Oh my God." Lea blinked. "Did you two go up in flames again?"

Sophia made the mistake of sucking in a breath while she still had a mouth full of cake. She began to cough, and tried not to think about going up in flames with Ryder.

That would be a mistake. A big mistake. Like sucking in a breath with a mouth full of cake.

"Was that shock? Or confirmation?" Lea studied her through narrowed eyes.

"Shock," Phoebe said, pushing a glass of water her way.

Elle nodded. "Yeah. Shock."

"Because you want to go up in flames." Lea grinned. "I'm an expert on that. Lord knows I pined after Ben most of my life, longing for that to happen." The astute woman tipped her head. "So, if not flames, then what? A kiss?"

A snort rippled up her throat.

"I think we have a winner." Elle smiled.

"You and Ryder kissed already?" Phoebe asked. "Is that why he left the restaurant the other day?"

This was getting out of hand.

She pushed her plate away. "No. We kissed after that. And I have no idea why he keeps throwing up this wall. One minute he's friendly, the next minute he's rude, then walks away."

"Wait." Lea blinked. "Did he also walk away after he kissed you?"

Now she sighed. "After the second kiss."

"There were two?" Phoebe's eyes widened.

Knowing the women were not going to let it rest, Sophia filled them in briefly on everything that happened that week. "I kind of feel like a yo-yo."

"He definitely has feelings for you," Elle said, sitting back.

"Yeah. He's in denial." Lea nodded. "Ben was like that with me. He was afraid to open up, and it caused him to do some stupid stuff, but it worked out in the end."

She held her friend's gaze. "I'm glad. But...I didn't come back here to reconnect with your brother. I'm here to help Phoebe. I'm here to work."

Sophia was getting tired of having to explain that to people. Just last night, she had to remind her mother of it again during their phone conversation.

"But you did reconnect, didn't you?" Phoebe asked.

She shrugged, not wanting to get into it.

"Well, then, ask yourself this." Lea leaned closer. "Do you like Ryder?"

"I…" She blew out a breath and recalled the laughter and heat they shared years ago, and how she'd returned to the city empowered. Her attitude had changed. Her outlook had changed. And because of that, her life had changed for the better. Ryder never pressured her, or complained. He seemed to like her for who she was, and it had been refreshing. She straightened her shoulders and nodded. "Yeah. I do like him. But, I wish he'd stop walking away."

"Then give him a reason to stay," Elle said, placing another piece of cake onto her empty one.

"What?" She blinked.

"Make him not want to leave." Lea set a hand on her shoulder. "Don't worry, I'm not going to talk sex, because this is my brother and…you know…eww. But, from what I just witnessed, and what you've just told us, he is fighting his attraction to you."

"Even if that were true, why bother? I'm only here for the summer," she said. "My life is in New York. His is here."

Laughing, Lea shrugged. "So? That's exactly how it is for me and Ben. But we're making it work. Quite well, actually."

"There's a difference though," she felt obliged to point out. "You and Ben love each other. Ryder and I, well, it's more of a physical type attraction." The kind where she wanted to rip his clothes off and lick every ridge, every muscle. Every inch. Twice. But, she couldn't tell his sister that, although, she was pretty sure, by the smirk on the woman's face, she knew.

"All the more reason for you to confront him the next time he tries to kiss and run." Lea grinned. "Pin his ass down."

A small flicker of disappointment fluttered through her belly. "I doubt there'll be a next time."

After the three women exchanged an amused look, they burst out laughing.

Why was that funny?

"Trust me," Lea said when she sobered. "There will definitely be a next time."

"Count on it."

"Definitely."

The other two said at once.

Sophia had no idea what made her friends so sure, and she couldn't help but wonder if perhaps they were right. Just the thought of locking lips with the guy again sent a delicious shiver down her spine.

Maybe she should consider their advice. After all, what harm could it do to go up in flames again?

Perhaps tomorrow, she'd test that theory.

Chapter Seven

By the time Ryder pulled into the theater parking lot, he'd secured one bid, and lost another…to that damn Colarusso Construction again. He got out of his truck and slammed the door.

It was getting old. Fast.

Tuesday, he was scheduled to give an estimate on a new flower shop coming to Main Street. It'd be great if he could land that one. Right now, though, he needed to concentrate on the theater, and helping secure some work for a few more college students.

Without his permission, warmth spread through his chest at the thought of Sophia, and the fact she not only wanted to help construction students, but some art students, too. Other than masking her eye color, there wasn't anything false about the woman. Or pretentious. She was a good person who genuinely wanted to help others achieve their dreams.

"Hey, Ryder." Ben exited the theater with a grin. "You here for your date?"

He reeled back. "My what?"

His buddy laughed, stopping in front of him. "Don't get your panties in a bunch. I'm just teasing you, man."

"Asshole." He shook his head.

"It's too bad, though," Ben said. "Sophia's great."

"Never said she wasn't."

His buddy nodded. "True. You prefer to put her in the not-going-there category. But we both know you've already gone there with her. You two have a history."

Aggravation prickled his spine. "Is there a reason we're talking about this?" He was having a hard enough time keeping memories of that weekend with Sophia at bay. Last thing he needed was his buddy stirring up the pot.

"Yeah. I like to yank your chain." Ben grinned.

"Why are you even here?" he asked.

"Because my girls are inside, and I wanted to see them before I headed down the Gap for drill weekend." Ben tipped his chin, daring him to find fault. "Oh, by the way, there's another reason I was talking to you about Sophia. It's because I'm a good friend. It's my duty to remind you of a time when that woman in there put a smile on your face for days. It'd be great to see it again. Especially since you're both unattached."

He grimaced. "Lea put you up to this, didn't she?"

"No." Ben shook his head. "It's all me. Your best buddy. The guy who thinks it's time you started to enjoy yourself again. Come on, Ryder. Not every woman is Jinan."

"Christ. Not that again."

"Yes, that again." Ben's gaze turned serious. "You've punished yourself enough. And for something that wasn't your fault. Let it go. Enjoy yourself. Enjoy Sophia."

How could he even contemplate being with such an amazing woman, when he'd let the woman he loved down? When he let her become a prisoner in a loveless marriage? He should've rescued her. Should've done more, instead of abiding by her wishes.

Last thing he needed was a woman in his life, messing with his head again.

"I'm not looking for a relationship, Ben." He hadn't gone down that road since Jinan.

His buddy chuckled. "Never said you were. And it's not what I was suggesting."

It wasn't? He frowned. "Then why are you pushing me toward Sophia?"

"Because, once-upon-a-time, you had fun with her. She made you laugh. Made you forget to be miserable."

True. The woman had certainly done that. A smile tugged his lips. "She's easy to be around."

"Then do it. Be around her. Enjoy her."

He scratched his temple. "She's only here for the summer."

"All the more reason to let go and enjoy the moment." Ben grinned.

Let go and enjoy the moment...

Something Ryder hadn't done in a long time. In fact, the last woman he'd ever let his guard down for was Sophia. And Ben was right, the no-strings woman had put a smile on his face long after she'd gone back to her life in the city.

But she'd also caused a few other thoughts to trickle into his brain. Like catching a train to visit her. Which—thank God—he'd never followed through on. Lord knew he hadn't been ready for anything like that back then.

Hell, he wasn't ready for that right now.

"No." He shook his head. "There's no reason to start anything. It's better that way."

And safer.

"Yeah. Heaven forbid you should have wild, no-strings-attached sex for a few months. That would be dumb." Ben nodded and slapped a hand on his shoulder. "Way to dodge that bullet, buddy." Then he walked to the parking lot laughing.

Asshole.

Ryder entered the building, shaking his head. His buddy was an idiot.

He also had a point.

What was to stop him and Sophia from picking up where they'd left off? Nothing but his survival instinct.

Too bad it was strong. And yelling at him to back away from the sexy New Yorker.

But as he walked into the design room, backing away from the woman was the last thing on his mind. He found her up on a ladder wearing cutoffs, boots, and a tank top that lifted up, exposing a strip of creamy skin.

Ah, hell. He was in big fucking trouble.

She wore a tool belt on her hips, emphasizing her curves, and he didn't think he'd seen anything so damn hot in his life. But it was the way she handled the drill in her hand that made him harder than the cinderblock wall she was drilling into.

Son-of-a-bitch...he was so screwed.

Somewhere in the back of his mind, he knew he should say something, or at the very least, get his mind out of the gutter—his sister and baby niece were in the building. Without realizing it, he'd moved closer, and damn...seeing those mile-long legs, and from that angle, reminded him of Sophia's flexibility, and one hell of an interesting position they'd explored in his former cabin.

He had several more he'd like to explore with her. Now.

As if sensing his presence, she stopped drilling and glanced down, rocking backward a little with a startled gasp. "Ryder. Sorry. Didn't know you were here."

Heart dropping into his stomach, he immediately grabbed the ladder. "Where's your spotter?"

"Excuse me?" She frowned down at him.

"Your spotter," he repeated, working to get his heartbeat back under control. "You shouldn't be on a ladder without one."

Her gaze narrowed a second before her chin lifted. "Well, you're here now. You can spot me while I finish up this last screw." And without waiting for him to reply, she turned around and completed securing a large whiteboard to the wall. "There." She grinned, elbow on her hip, drill in her hand, looking so at-ease with the tool, he wondered if she slept with the damn thing under her pillow.

And because he had a tool he'd love for her to handle, he forced the dangerous thought from his mind and tried to pretend nothing was wrong. "You can come down now."

Her grin increased. "I know. I kind of like this angle."

Her playful tone did funny things to his chest.

"Me, too." He let his gaze trail slowly up her bare legs. "But if you don't get down, I won't be responsible for what others might stumble on if they walked in here."

Heaven help him, a wicked gleam entered her eyes and she stepped down a few rungs, putting him eye-level with the promised land.

"Is that better?"

Fuck, yeah. That was great. And he would've told her, but he forgot how to speak. His mind fogged over. No doubt because he had no blood left in his brain. He shook his head, trying to clear it.

Didn't work.

She stepped down onto the next rung. "Or would you rather this?"

His gaze was now even with mouth-watering cleavage, two beautiful breasts, and a pair of pert nipples, visible under her top, telling him she was just as aroused.

None of that helped his situation.

He swallowed past his dry throat and forced his gaze to meet hers. "This isn't smart."

"True." She nodded and came down the rest of the way.

It would've been good, except for the fact he still held onto the ladder. With a death grip. It was ironic how his defense for keeping his hands off her did little to keep hers off him.

Palms on his chest, she hesitated, and he found himself holding his breath to see if she was going to push him away or pull him close. God help him, he was equally terrified of both.

Chapter Eight

Gaze still glued to his, she trembled against him. Unaware of how it happened, Ryder had her trapped between the ladder and his body, as he continued to grip the sides. But he failed to resist dipping down to drag his mouth up her throat.

"This is a bad idea," he murmured against her skin, loving how she sucked in a breath and clutched his shirt.

"Then this is probably bad, too," she muttered a second before rocking into him.

Damn, that felt good.

She must've thought so too, because she did it again. And yet again.

His mouth was halfway across her jaw, needing to taste her hot kiss when he heard a voice approaching in the hall.

Shit. Lea.

Pushing away from the ladder, he took several steps back from Sophia's sweet body just as his sister walked in, cradling her baby.

"Good. I caught you." Lea smiled.

Unsure of her meaning, he decided to ignore it, and focused instead on his cute niece. "Wow, Lea, every time I see Melody, she's grown."

"I know. I'm afraid to blink." His sister smiled, walking up to him with the baby. "Want to hold her?"

He held his hands up and stepped back. "No. Not a good idea. Think I'll wait until she's walking around before I attempt that."

"Well, I'd love to hold her," Sophia said, stepping close. "She's even more beautiful in person, Lea."

"Thank you." His sister carefully transferred her daughter to the smiling woman.

"You are just a cutie pie, aren't you?" Sophia cradled his niece, talking soft and sweet as she gently rocked back and forth.

An ache appeared in his chest and intensified the longer he watched the beautiful woman holding the tiny baby. He was having trouble breathing. And dammit, now his ears were ringing.

"Are you going to get that?" his sister asked, pointing to his pocket. "Your phone?"

Phone?

Right. Damn. *That* was what was ringing. He pulled it from his pocket and answered on his way to the hall, hoping it hadn't disturbed his niece too much. "Yeah?"

"Ryder? You there, Son?" His father's voice hit his ear.

He stilled. "Yeah. What's wrong? Are you okay?"

"I'm fine. It's that stupid door to the stock room. It fell off."

Closing his eyes, he rubbed his temple and quickly ran his schedule through his brain. "I have two meetings this morning. Can you put it aside?" he asked, opening his eyes. "I'll stop by sometime this afternoon."

"That'll work," his dad said. "Thanks. Sorry to take you away from work."

He frowned. "It's okay, Dad. Don't ever hesitate to call."

"Thanks, Son. I'll see you later."

The line went dead. Ryder shoved the phone back in his pocket and re-entered the room. Once again, his chest took a direct blow.

Sophia stood there with the sweetest, softest look on her face as she lowered her head to brush her lips over the baby's forehead. She'd make a great mom. The woman was caring and fun. Someone you could count on.

Unlike him.

His stomach rippled as if punched. What the hell was he doing with her? He had no business messing with someone so nice.

Too nice for the likes of him.

From now on, he was going to have to make sure he was never in this room with her alone. It was jinxed. Or an enabler. Both times he'd found himself alone with the woman he'd been unable to keep his lips off her.

Not going to happen again.

***

Sophia wasn't sure if it was the phone call or his sister's presence that caused the change in Ryder. He'd left room as *Mr. I'm-going-to-knock-your-socks-off*, but returned as *Mr. Indifferent*.

Dammit.

Just when she thought she'd gotten through, he closed up. Too bad, because she'd made progress, playfully peeling away a few layers to get to the man she'd had fun with years ago. For a few minutes, he'd appeared, burning her up from the inside out.

Now, it was square one all over again.

"You're obviously no stranger to children," Lea said, regaining her attention.

She smiled down at the cutie in her arms. "True. My oldest brother has a little girl who's three and a little boy who's one. I helped my sister-in-law out as much as possible when my brother was deployed."

"What branch is he in?" Ryder asked.

"Marines," she replied. "At least, he was. He resigned his commission."

Lea nodded. "That'll be easier on his wife. I don't look forward to Ben leaving in March."

"He'll be fine," Ryder said, stepping close to brush his finger over the baby's soft hair. "You all will."

A lump the size of a cinderblock lodged itself in Sophia's throat. It didn't take much for her to imagine him looking so tenderly at his own baby.

Whoa. Now that was a dangerous thought.

"Hey, guys. Look over here," Lea said, and when Sophia and Ryder glanced at her, the woman snapped a picture. "Thanks. I want to send it to Brandi."

She gave herself a mental shake. Time to give the baby back to her momma, and get to work. "Thanks for bringing Melody here for me to meet her."

"No problem." Lea held out her arms, and Sophia handed over the yawning baby, who started to fuss. "She got to see her uncle Ryder, too."

A smile actually curved his mouth, but he remained silent.

"Are you leaving now?" Sophia asked. "We can walk you out. I just need to change quickly before we head to the college."

"Thanks, but it's almost time to nurse her," Lea said. "So, if you don't mind, I might stick around in here to do that before I leave."

"Of course." She unfolded a metal chair and set it by the table for Lea, then grabbed the folder with her sketches and shoved them in her purse. "Ready?" she asked Ryder. "I left my dress in the lobby bathroom, so I could change on the way out."

When he nodded and motioned with his hand for her to lead the way, she grabbed her purse and headed out the door. He was very quiet.

Too quiet.

Not at all like the sexy man, pressing her against the ladder with his hot, hard body.

But somehow, someway, she was determined to peel those layers back and free *Mr. Knock-your-socks-off*, whether Ryder liked it or not.

***

Almost a week had passed since Ryder was alone with Sophia. In any room. He told himself it was a good thing. It kept him from making a mistake they might both regret. Although, every time he found himself recalling their embraces, the only regret he had was not spending more time with her—alone.

Overall, he'd seen her four times that week. Three were at the theater, and one was lunch at the diner with the gang. Each time, they'd been surrounded by people. Safe. No chance of screwing up again.

But that didn't stop him from thinking about it. Hell, no. Especially when she paired those shorts with boots and that sexy tool belt. Even now, his veins heated just thinking about her luscious silhouette.

But luckily, they'd had volunteers to guide. And so far, things were going great in that department. His team was constructing the sets, her team was painting them and adding details. It was a good system. They already had one set completely finished, and half of another.

But, he wasn't going to think about the theater. Wasn't going to think about Sophia. He wasn't even going to think about work, even though, by some miracle, he'd managed to win both bids that week. Nope. Tonight, he was going to concentrate on enjoying the Mets game with Ethan and Ben on Ethan's big screen TV. It was the closest thing to actually being at the game.

It was Thursday, so the women were out having their chocolate fest, which left their husbands free to enjoy sports, like back in the old days.

Smiling, he carried three boxes of pizza—his one addiction—through the resort, to a special entrance Brandi had created for the Wyne family's private residence section. He shifted the boxes to one hand and knocked on the door. Man, he could almost taste the cold beer in Ethan's fridge. But it wasn't Ethan who answered the door. It was Phoebe.

"Hey, Ryder. Come on in." She smiled and stepped aside, wearing a pretty black dress.

He raised a brow. "Hi, Phoebe. You look nice. Didn't expect to see you here. Was your chocolate thing canceled?" He entered, but waited for her to proceed him down the hall that led to the open-concept kitchen family room.

She laughed. "Sort of."

An uneasy feeling crept up his spine, then branched out over his shoulders when they reached the family room. Ethan and Ben were there, without T-shirt, jeans, and beer. They wore suits, and stood next to his sister—also wearing a black dress.

"What's going on?" He walked further into the room, where he noticed Sophia, leaning against the kitchen island near a bottle of wine and large chocolate cake with cherries on top. Her hair was down and fell in waves over her bare shoulders. Awareness spread through him at sickening speed. She wore a dress too, but not a fancy black one. It was a casual one, with flowers printed all over.

He had the urge to pick each and every one.

She smirked. "We've been dumped for a show."

"Not dumped, exactly," Lea said, coming closer. "Phoebe managed to snag tickets last minute to Hamilton. And Ben and I haven't been out together without the baby since she was born, so…we have to go. We need to go."

Ben walked over and slipped an arm around his wife. "Whatever she wants, she gets."

"Feel free to stay here and watch the game, though," Ethan told him, moving to his wife's side.

Phoebe turned to Sophia. "Same with you. Enjoy the wine and chocolate. Elle wasn't going to make it tonight anyway, so I sent some over to her, too. There was no need for either of you to miss out."

"Thanks." Sophia nodded. "Enjoy the show. It's amazing."

Lea's eyes rounded. "Oh my God, did you get to see Lin perform?"

She nodded. "Yes. He was fantastic."

Ryder had no idea what they were talking about, and he could tell by the way his buddies' eyes glazed over they joined him in the clueless population.

"I did, too. But I'm excited to see it again," Phoebe said, hooking her arm through her husband's. "We should get going or we'll miss the first act."

Twenty seconds later, he stood in the family room alone, staring at Sophia.

"So, that just happened," she said with a grin. "What game were you here to watch?"

"Mets."

Her eyes widened. "The Mets are on tonight? Sweet." Grinning, she grabbed the wine and cake, then moved to the fridge, where she managed to grab a beer. "Keiffer's TV isn't quite as big as this one." She nodded toward the gorgeous monster on the wall. "But, you're more than welcome to come up and watch the game with me. I'll even share some of my chocolate, if you'll give up a few slices of that pizza."

"You like the Mets?" he asked inanely.

She snickered. "Hello? I'm from Queens. Of course, I love the Mets." Grin still in place, she strode past him and headed up the stairs. Halfway there, she turned to look over her shoulder at him. "Are you coming?"

Because he wanted to come with her...literally, he knew he should tell her no. It was the smart thing to do. Watching the game with her, in a private townhouse, with their out-of-control chemistry, was not a good idea. It was a bad one. In fact, it was downright dumb.

So why did he nod and ascend the stairs behind her?

Because he was fucking stupid.

Chapter Nine

No, it was because she had the beer and the TV, and the game started in four minutes, he silently argued with himself. And he continued to stick to that as they sat on her couch and enjoyed the food and drink and first five innings of the game.

"Ah, come on, ump." She shot to her feet. "He was out. Are you kidding me?" Her eyes blazed as she turned to him, mouth open, brow furrowed. "Do you believe that?

What he couldn't believe was how strong the urge was to pull her onto his lap and suck her full lower lip into his mouth. She must've read some of it in his eyes, because her demeanor changed from outraged to aroused.

Her breathing changed, too, as if breath clogged her throat. She sank back down on the couch and blinked at him. "Ryder." She cleared her throat. "You shouldn't look at me like that."

"Like what?"

"Like you want to ravage me from head to toe."

A smile tugged his lips, as he lost his mind and reached for her. "I was thinking toe to head."

"That's different then," she said, reaching for him too, gaze locked on his mouth.

Once again, he could tell she wanted it on hers. And because that was exactly what he'd wanted, he ignored the alarm bells going off in his head, and closed the remaining distance between them.

Her flowery scent filled his nostrils, increasing the heat already coursing through his body. Sliding his hands up into her hair, he held her where he wanted her and skimmed his mouth over her jaw, grazing her skin with his teeth, before capturing her sigh in a kiss he'd wanted to take for days.

Lazy, deep, tasting her in slow, thorough sweeps that had her trembling in his arms. He missed this. Missed the crazy, all-consuming out-of-control need she invoked, and the way she responded in kind. Her hands were in his hair now, and her tongue met his in a hungry, wild manner, driving him fucking insane. He had to be insane to be kissing her again.

Christ…what was he doing?

Stiffening, he broke the kiss, pushed her aside and stood. "Damn, Sophia. I'm sorry." He backed up a few feet and worked to get his breathing under control. "I shouldn't have done that. I came here to watch the game, not…"

"What?" She rose to her feet and held his gaze. "Not kiss me like you can't get enough."

He nodded. "Yeah. That."

Her dress was askew, a good portion of one of her gorgeous breasts bared where his hands longed to stray.

"It's funny," she said, regaining his attention. "Never took you for a coward."

A coward?

Frowning, he reeled back. "What are you talking about?"

She folded her arms across her chest, plumping up her delicious curves. The lower part of his anatomy was still cocked. Now it was loaded.

"You're running away again." Her shrewd gaze locked onto him.

He narrowed his eyes. "Is that what you think I'm doing?"

"Aren't you?"

"No." He thrust a hand through his hair. "I'm trying to save you."

She reeled back. "Save me from what?"

"Me."

Her features softened, and she moved close, with a determined gleam in her eyes. "Ryder?"

"Yeah?" He tried to step back, but an armchair prevented his escape.

"I'll let you in on a little secret." Her palms met his chest, and his heartbeat thundered in his ears.

"What?"

"I don't want to be saved from you."

His heart rocked in his chest. Her confession made it hard for him to remain strong. Even his body was already caving, because his hand rose to brush a strand of hair back from her face. "Sophia, I'm not a forever kind of guy."

Instead of stiffening, or pushing him away, she smiled at him, and spread her fingers on his chest. "That's good, since I'm leaving here in a little over two months."

"What are you saying?" He needed to be sure, because his interpretation sounded too good to be true.

"I'm not looking for forever, either." Again, she smiled, but this time, she emphasized her words by rocking against him. "Is there anything else we need to clear up before you kiss me like you can't get enough?"

The last of his misgivings disappeared under the sexy invitation in her eyes. "Nope."

He cupped her face and gave her what she wanted, what he wanted, too. Hungrily, and deeply, he feasted on her taste, sweeping his tongue inside her mouth to reacquaint himself with her essence.

She moaned and slid her hands under his shirt, stroking his abs in soft, circular motions. Damn, that felt good. And when she unhooked his jeans and slid the zipper part way down, he groaned, needing to feel her hands around him.

But not yet. He'd never last.

Releasing her lips, he dragged his mouth down her throat, while his hands made quick work of her dress, tugging it all the way down her trembling curves. He stepped back and watched the material fall to her feet, and everything inside him tightened at once.

She kicked off her sandals, and wiggled out of her lacy underwear, until she stood before him, completely naked.

"God, you're so beautiful, Sophia." Even more than he'd remembered.

Donna Michaels

He ran his hands up the curve of her waist, across her ribs to brush his palms over her pert nipples.

"Ryder…" Her voice was low, strained, needy.

So was he. All of him.

Dipping down, he captured a beauty in his mouth, while rolling the other between his thumb and forefinger.

She gripped his head and cried out, pressing her body into him. He switched sides, enthralled by her moans and the way her breath hitched in her throat. If it weren't for the need ripping through him, he'd gladly continue to drive her wild. Drive them both wild.

But he needed more. Needed to taste her.

He dropped to his knees and kissed a path over her quivering belly, while he slid his hands up her legs. "You might want to sit for this," he said, gently pushing her down into the arm chair.

Caressing the soft skin behind her knees, he bent down to brush open-mouthed kisses up her inner thigh. She spread her legs, and the view took his breath. For the first time in his life, Ryder wasn't sure he could hold on.

But he had to. He had to taste her. To make her cry out in a pleasure too strong to contain.

Using the pad of his finger, he stroked her center, finding her wet and ready, and his erection throbbed behind his half-opened zipper.

"Ryder," she whispered, breathing already unsteady. "How soundproof are these walls?"

82

"Very. Besides, Mason's townhouse is empty next door." Anticipation upped his pulse, because he knew why she was asking.

Sophia gripped his shoulders and smiled. "Good, because I could never be quiet with you."

"No need," he murmured against her thigh, and holding her gaze, dark with need, he slid his finger inside.

She cried out and thrust forward, "I...I'm not going to last."

"Good." He slid his finger in and out. "Let me know how much you like it," he urged, before placing his mouth on her too.

A low, sexy, sound ripped from her throat. "Yes. That's g-good...so good." Her grip on his shoulders tightened. "Don't stop."

Not an option.

She was fucking perfect. Her little moans, and loud cries, they all filled him with an inner peace he could never explain.

Changing the angle, he upped his strokes and watched her head fall back as she tightened around him and let out the sexiest, loud, needy moan he'd ever heard.

Clenching his jaw to keep from following her over, he prolonged her orgasm with a series of quicker strokes. When her cries eventually stopped, he slowed his thrusts, watching her come back to earth. Her body went limp and she slumped against the back of the chair.

She was magnificent.

He released her and stood to quickly shed the rest of his clothes.

"Wow, Ryder." She sucked in a ragged breath, satisfaction glowing in her gaze. "That was even more intense than I remember."

Fishing out a nearly expired condom from his jeans, he smiled down at her. "We're nowhere near done."

Chapter Ten

Sophia's pulse still hammered in her chest as she watched Ryder roll a condom onto a big, mouthwatering erection that was the cause of many fond memories. And damn, she was so ready to make more. Her body heated, despite the fact she still trembled with aftershocks from a fierce orgasm he just gave that robbed her strength.

Ryder was even more magnificent than she remembered. Muscles and ridges graced his body, and he had a sexy sprinkling of hair that crisscrossed down his abs right through the middle of that sexy Vee of his that drove her nuts.

Suddenly rejuvenated, she rose to her feet and took him in her hand. "Let me help."

He pulsed, and her body responded in kind. *Sweet mercy.* It was amazing how much she already ached for him. The restraint he showed was remarkable. He shook, but didn't make a move to touch her.

She released him and drew in a breath as his eyes met hers, deliciously dark and hungry. God, could she relate. His flesh gleamed in the soft glow of the lamps, and flickering light of the television.

They stared for a beat, then lunged at each other, touching, stroking, caressing every inch in a frenzy of moves, like they wanted to touch everywhere at once. She certainly did. His mouth was hot and demanding on hers, stoking the fire he'd started several minutes ago.

"Sophia," he murmured after releasing her mouth to place kisses down her throat. "Missed this." His voice was thrillingly gruff.

She used her mouth to get reacquainted with his body, tracing her tongue over his collarbone, a pec, flicking a nipple, eliciting a rough groan from deep in his chest she felt clear into hers. "Me, too."

Sucking in a sharp breath, he threaded his hands in her hair and covered her mouth with his again, which worked for her because his kisses were amazing. It was long and wet and deep, and she trembled with pure need, while returning the favor. Warm, deliciously rough hands, sent a thrill through her when they left her hair to cup her breasts and his wicked fingertips teased her nipples. It was as if he remembered just exactly how she liked it.

In a swift move, he cupped her ass to lift her up. "Wrap your legs around me," he said, and walked the two feet to the nearest wall as she obeyed the quiet command.

She moaned at the sheer pleasure of brushing his erection where she ached the most. A second later, her back met the wall. "Cold," she squeaked.

"Not for long," he said against her neck. "But this first time is going to be fast. We're too combustible."

"Good," she said, cupping his face, forcing him to meet her gaze. "Because I'm about ready to burst."

The need darkening his gaze clogged the breath in her throat.

"Wait for me." He gripped her hips and brushed her center with the tip of his erection.

Sophia gasped. "Yes." She rocked against him, urging him to move.

Needing no further instruction, Ryder thrust deep with one sure, shocking push, filling her to the hilt, and memories from years ago flooded her senses.

That...*that* was what she missed. Pure bliss.

Gasping in tandem pleasure, they stared at each other a beat.

"God, Sophia." His gaze smoldered. "Even better than I remembered."

She sucked in a breath. "Me, too."

Heaven help her, she'd never felt anything so intense, so achingly incredible, with anyone but this man. He filled her completely. The perfect fit.

Bending down, he kissed the curve of her neck, sending goose bumps down her side. He tightened his grip on her hips and began to move. Her whole body tingled. She was close. So blessedly close to that blissful edge again.

She moaned and arched closer. He scraped his thumb over her, just above where they were joined. That was it. All it took. She cried out, arching against him as she burst into a million and one pieces. He threw his head back, gripped her hips, and drove hard and deep inside her, muttering her name as he followed her with his own release.

***

Sun streaked through the blinds in a three-slice pattern on the floor as Ryder woke up from one of the best nights he'd ever had…might even have topped his epic New Year's Eve. It was no wonder since the same woman was the reason behind both historic nights. Turning over, he reached for Sophia, but the bed was empty.

The sound of the shower shutting off sent a rush of heat through his body at the memory of her kneeling down, grasping his hips, while working him over until she'd melted every last bone in his body.

"Good morning." She smiled, breezing into the room, wrapped in a towel, just like that day he'd walked in on her.

But unlike that day, he wasn't running away from the need and awareness she sparked in him.

"Good morning." He got out of bed and strode to her, thrilled when she met him halfway. Pushing her wet hair off her shoulder, he bent down to kiss a path to her ear. "Why didn't you wake me up?"

It was funny how much had changed in a little over a week. But it was a good change. A welcome change.

She hadn't kicked him out of her bed. Nor had she asked him to stay. The amazing woman left that all up to him. After the way they'd combusted in her living room, he never even thought about leaving her last night.

"I was worried that perhaps I'd worn you out." She skimmed her hands down his torso, brushing her thumbs across his abs, causing them to quiver.

"You know," he said against her wet skin. "If you reach a little lower, I think you'll find I'm far from worn out."

Laughing, she did just that. "So it would seem."

He bit the curve of her neck and rocked into her hand. "Nothing fake about it."

"Mmm…" Tipping her head, she gave him better access, while her fingers grew bolder, stroking him full tilt. "It's a shame I have to go to work."

Reaching between them, he slipped his fingers into her cleavage, gave a quick tug, and her towel fell onto their feet. "You can't go just yet," he said, sweeping her into his arms.

"Why not?" Her playful gaze sparkled beneath a raised brow.

He fucking loved that he was staring into one brown eye and one blue eye. Loved that they both stripped away all pretense and came at each other without anything to hide.

"Because." He set her on the covers, then grasped her ankles and spread her legs. "It's time for breakfast in bed."

***

For most of the day—okay, for all of the day—Sophia walked around with a smile on her face. She couldn't help it. She was happy. Content. Satisfied. All thanks to Ryder.

Her mind revisited the amazing things the man had done to her last night…and this morning, and heat rushed through her tired and sore body. And just like that, she was instantly rejuvenated, which was good. She was on her own today, but Ryder and the college students were scheduled to help tomorrow and Sunday.

Today she was feeling inspired, so she started work on painting one of the background scenes. She was halfway done when Phoebe breezed into the area backstage where the sets were built and stored.

"Hey, Sophia."

"Hi. What's up?" she asked, setting her paintbrush down. "Will I be in your way during rehearsal tonight?"

Phoebe shook her head. "No. You're fine here." Her gaze narrowed, and mouth twitched. "I wanted to apologize for leaving you in the lurch last night, but something tells me it's not necessary."

"You'd be correct." She grinned. Couldn't help it.

Dammit.

Her friend leaned against a ladder, a smile spreading across her face. "Anything to do with a certain, good-looking carpenter from your past?"

She nodded. "It has a lot do with him."

"That's great. But what changed?"

"He did," she replied. "He finally realized I wasn't going to make any demands on him. That I wasn't looking for forever."

They had commitments. People depending on them. Lived in two different states. The list was endless.

Phoebe cocked her head. "You going to be okay spending time with him, then leaving at the end of the summer?"

"Yeah." She lifted a shoulder. "Why not? I left him before."

"But you'd only spent two days together." Phoebe shook her head. "That's a lot different than two months."

She waved a hand. "It'll be fine. I already know going in that it's just a summer fling thing. And that makes a difference."

"I hope you're right." Phoebe sighed, gaze not so convinced. "I don't want to see you get hurt."

"Thanks," she said, doing her best to reassure her friend. "I don't have time to get hurt. I have more productions to help you with, besides this one. Plus, South Pacific renderings to produce."

Phoebe pushed from the ladder and nodded. "Then I won't keep you, especially from this background. It already looks amazing, Sophia."

"Thanks," she said again.

Glad to have pleased her boss, she picked up her paintbrush and continued…with a smile on her face.

***

It was July 1st, and Ryder sat on Ethan's deck, enjoying a beer with him, Jeremy, and Ben, while the women were all at tonight's show. He had no idea where June had gone. It flew by. *Because you had fun*, his mind supplied. That was, indeed, true. A smile tugged his lips. They'd finished the sets early last week, and the show opened last night.

Sophia was already halfway through designing sets for the youth production of Grease, and he looked forward to start helping with them over the weekend. It was amazing to watch her creativity and expertise at work.

"There he goes, smiling again," Jeremy said, with a roll of his eyes.

Used to the teasing by now, he just flipped him off and drank his beer.

"You're just envious because he's getting some and you aren't," Ben said, slouching while his baby girl slept on his chest.

Ever since that night he and Sophia watched the Mets and...combusted, Ryder had garnered a different outlook. He stopped hesitating where she was concerned. If he wanted to see her on days he wasn't volunteering at the theater, he stopped in to see her. If he wanted to have lunch with her, he brought her lunch. Or they met at Timbers Grille in the resort, or his dad's restaurant, or sometimes, they even met at her place and had a really great lunch.

She never seemed to mind, either. In fact, he got the impression she would be happy to see him every day. Which was great, except he craved her company every day too, and he didn't want forever.

Because of that, he made a point to go a day or two without exposure to her sweetness. It was also the reason he had yet to bring her to his house. They only had sex in her bed.

But, he was beginning to realize that wasn't fair. And that it put a selfish spin on their fun.

"Wait a minute." Jeremy reeled back. "Who said I'm not getting any?"

Ben smirked. "Does that mean you're giving the pretty author something to write about besides parking tickets?"

Ryder's chuckle mixed with Ethan's, and this time it was Jeremy who waved his middle finger.

"I think that's a negatory." Ethan grinned.

"That's too bad," he said, holding up his hand and wiggling his fingers. "Because a date with Rosey Palmer and her five sisters doesn't count."

Jeremy snorted. "Fuck you, Ryder."

"I wouldn't want to make Rosey jealous." He laughed, and the others joined in.

"Or Sophia," Ben said.

Ethan nodded. "You've been seeing her a lot, Ryder. And that's a good thing."

"Yeah." Ben's tone turned serious. "She's good for you. You're happy. Content."

Jeremy leaned forward and held his gaze. "They're right. All kidding aside, it's good to see you giving yourself a break. It's about damn time."

Not one for touchy-feely moments with the guys, especially when they're directed at him, Ryder lifted his beer in a mock toast and drank. It was much safer to keep his feelings buried than to confront them. The last time he'd done that he'd gotten burnt.

Yeah, it was definitely much safer to keep things light and physical with Sophia.

The Fourth of July was in a couple of days. It was time for some fun that wasn't so selfish. A special plan started to formulate in his mind. With luck, they'd make that holiday memorable, too.

Chapter Eleven

Sophia wasn't sure what to expect when she received a text from Ryder to meet him at the dock behind Ethan's house, with a bathing suit and an overnight bag. The invitation and mystery sent a scintillating shiver down her body. Nothing was ever dull with him.

Smiling, she grabbed her bag and headed downstairs for breakfast with Phoebe and Ethan, wearing her bikini under one of her summer dresses.

"Morning, sunshine," Phoebe said, then narrowed her eyes. "Ooh, what's that smile for, and the overnight bag?"

She greeted her hosts then told them about Ryder's invitation as she sat down at the table and started to eat her plate of eggs and bacon.

"Well…I'll be." Ethan stopped buttering a bagel and grinned. "He's going to take you to his house."

"His house?" Her heart tripped. She thought maybe they were going to spend the day on the lake, then perhaps camp in the woods or something.

Ethan nodded, continuing to butter his bagel while she continued to eat. "To my knowledge, he's never taken a woman there before. This is a good thing."

A strange fluttering filled her chest.

"Good?" Phoebe's brows rose, and face lit up. "It's a great thing. You're really loosening him up, Sophia. I haven't known Ryder as long as the Wynes, but it doesn't take a genius to recognize he's a closed-up workaholic."

That broke her heart. Mostly because she'd noticed the same thing her first day here.

"You brought fun back into his life," Ethan said. "Ben and I were talking about it last week." He lifted his glass of orange juice in a toasting manner. "Great job, Sophia. Keep doing whatever you're doing."

Other than working together, laughing a lot, and sleeping together, she wasn't doing anything special. Just having the *fun* he'd mentioned.

"I think it's safe to say it goes both ways." Phoebe glanced from her husband to her. "Seems to me Ryder's brought some fun into your life, too."

She smiled. "Yes, it's safe to say that."

And a lot of heat, too.

"Well, since we have today off for the holiday, I think it would be great if you took tomorrow night off too," Phoebe said. "Your assistants can take care of any prop mishaps, and you're already way ahead on the Grease renderings, so enjoy yourself. That's an order."

Sophia sat up straight and saluted. "Yes, ma'am."

Laughter echoed around the table, and it wasn't long before she received another text from Ryder with an ETA of five minutes. She finished the last of her bacon and the rest of her coffee, then stood.

"I'd better get to the dock. Thanks for breakfast," she said, grabbing her dishes.

"Leave them." Phoebe waved. "I'll clean up. Just go have fun."

She nodded. "Thanks. And as for taking tomorrow night off, I don't know. It depends on Ryder. I'm not sure what he has planned. Maybe he's going to bring me back in the afternoon."

Ethan chuckled. "Trust me, he'll be happy to have you stay another night."

"So, there." Phoebe nodded, smirk twitching her lips. "I'll see you on the 6th."

With a smile on her face, she left the Wynes and rushed through their yard, down to the dock. The sun was shining in a cloudless sky. Picnic perfect weather. She stood with her hand to her forehead, shielding her eyes while she scoured the lake for Ryder.

Several boats were already crisscrossing the water with people eager to get a jump on the holiday. She was kind of eager to jump something else.

Lordy, she was so easy when it came to Ryder. No other man made her want to have sex all the damn time. It was exhausting and amazing, and she was definitely going to miss him when she got back to reality and her life in New York City.

Dropping her hand from her face, she tightened her grip on her bag and smiled as a boat neared the dock. Right now, reality could go jump in the lake. An amazing, mysterious day lay ahead of her, and dammit, she wasn't going to let anything ruin it.

"Morning," she said, as he slowed to a crawl and maneuvered his sleek boat close to the dock.

He was sheer perfection in jeans, a navy T-shirt that hugged his perfectly toned muscles, and a pair of aviator sunglasses that were sexy-as-sin and gave him a hint of danger.

Damn, he was hot.

Tough, powerful, he appeared almost unapproachable, but she still harbored that rebellious streak, and it gave her the courage to be brave, bold, to tread where others backed off.

"Good morning." He smiled, and damn, it outshined the sun. "Toss me your bag." He kept one hand on the wheel and held out the other.

She did as she was told, her heart starting to hammer in her chest. "You're not going to tie it down?"

"Nope." He grinned. "You're going to hop in."

Yeah, probably gracelessly into the water.

"Don't worry. I've got you." He held his hand out to her.

Well...let the fun begin, she thought as she leaned down, grasped his hand and jumped.

Of course, she landed without incident in his boat. The man was too capable to let anything else happen. And very hard and warm.

She slid her hands around Ryder, who caught her with his body. "Good morning," she said again, softer this time, tipping her head back in an open invitation.

"It is now," he murmured before capturing her mouth for a slow, thorough kiss that knocked her off-kilter. When he released her mouth, he smiled down at her. "Ready?"

For anything. "Yes. Where do you want me?"

His grin increased. "I have a few places in mind, but for now, you can sit there." He motioned to the chair next to him.

Turned on beyond measure, she was happy to sink onto the cushions, since her legs were suddenly rubber.

"Here. These are for you." He handed her a pair of sunglasses and a lifejacket.

She put the glasses on but frowned at the vest. "I can swim."

"You can also drown." His tone turned serious. "Not with me."

"You're not wearing one," she pointed out.

He folded his arms across his chest and lowered his chin. "Please put it on."

She smiled at him and shrugged into the vest. "Since you asked nicely."

His lips twitched. "Thank you."

"You're welcome," she said. "You can make it up to me later."

"Count on it," he said, with more heat in his tone than was blaring down on her from the sky, and her good parts perked up in response.

She loved his potent, commanding side.

Once she was secured, he maneuvered the boat backward and away from the dock, before heading the way he'd come. She watched him from behind the protection of her glasses. Potent was too soft a word. A force of nature maybe? Definitely intoxicating, because just looking at him made her dizzy with need and turned up the flame on slow burn in her belly.

Too noisy for conversation since he opened up the throttle, she sat back, closed her eyes, and enjoyed the feel of the sun on her face while her mind remained on Ryder.

He was fast becoming her favorite addiction. A necessity. Which wasn't smart for a *not* forever thing. But it was what it was. She felt what she felt. And she wondered if perhaps he had the same thoughts about her.

As the boat started to slow down, she opened her eyes and nearly lost her breath. Miles of pristine woods met her gaze, and nestled between the trees was a wooden structure too large to be considered a cabin, and too gorgeous for words.

A boathouse sat on a long dock with steps that led to a huge deck running the length of the house. Gorgeous, floor to ceiling, two-story windows reflected the sun. Two smaller, private decks hugged the side of the house where she assumed the bedrooms were located on the second floor.

After backing the boat into the boathouse, Ryder cut the engine and secured the boat to an inner dock. "Give me your glasses," he said, then stowed both pair in a compartment in front of her seat, before tossing her bag onto the dock. "I'll get out first, then help you."

"Okay." She watched the muscles in his arm bunch as he grabbed a post and jumped out. He made it look so easy. She reached for the buckle on her vest, but he shook his head.

"Leave it on," he said, thrusting his hand toward her.

He was very protective, very worried about her well-being. Unable to fault him for that, she kept it on, and embraced the warmth his caring created as she took his hand and he hoisted her next to him.

"Welcome to my house."

Chapter Twelve

Her heart shifted in her chest. Ethan was right. Ryder had taken her to his home, and not someplace he rented for the night.

Maybe she was starting to mean more to him than just sex. Great sex.

For something that should've been bad, considering her temporarily-in-the-Poconos status, it felt damn good.

She smiled. "Thanks for bringing me here."

His gaze was friendly and a little bit heated as he unhooked her buckle and brushed her nipples as he slowly removed her vest. "My pleasure."

The way her nipples pebbled at his touch, it was obvious it was her pleasure, too.

He dropped the vest back into the boat, then ran his finger along her temple and down her jaw before lowering his mouth to hers. It was one of his long, slow, thorough kisses, that stole her breath, melted her bones, made her ache for him.

Breaking the kiss, he stared into her eyes. "I can't think when my mouth is on you. We'd better save that for later. I want to give you the tour."

Happy for the promise of later, and for the tour, she smiled. "Lead the way."

He hoisted her bag on his shoulder, grabbed her hand, then led her out of the boat house and onto the main dock. Standing there, looking up at the house, she lost her breath again.

It was even more magnificent up close.

"You built this too, didn't you?"

His head turned to her, and a flash of wonder entered his eyes. "How can you tell?"

She smiled at the clueless man. "It's as unique as your signature or thumbprint. You have a style, Ryder. An incredible style that…speaks to me. I don't know, I just feel it." Goose bumps spread down her arm in confirmation. "There's a strength, a distinctive approach. Your use of lines, and attention to detail, all of it screams you."

"A guy who's addicted to pizza and a certain someone's kisses?" he teased.

Fighting a grin, she nodded. "Exactly."

He laughed, and the pure sound reignited her goose bumps. "Come on. I'll show you the inside. Maybe you can tell what I like for breakfast by the way I designed the kitchen."

"You're on." She already knew what he liked for breakfast, and it wasn't food.

All through the tour, his playful manner remained. The open-concept first floor had a vaulted ceiling, with those gorgeous windows, and an amazing stone fireplace along one wall. His kitchen was to die for, with state of the art appliances, granite counters, and a huge walk-in pantry. The man had created her dream kitchen.

It was mouthwatering, like him.

Upstairs were three bedrooms and two bathrooms. One bedroom was dedicated for his sister's nephew Tyler. The other, she assumed, would eventually accommodate his niece...once she was walking. Then there was the master. Large. Incredible. It had a king size bed, that made her stomach flutter, another gorgeous stone fireplace, and an equally impressive bathroom. The double sinks and jetted tub were amazing, but the huge stone wall, walk-in shower, with a bench and a big showerhead in the ceiling made her gasp. She forced herself to exit the bathroom before she gave into the urge to strip him naked then and there.

More floor-to-ceiling windows covered the back wall, and when he slid them wide open, it lent new meaning to bringing the outdoors inside. But the best part of the private deck was the... "Hot tub?"

"Yes." He brushed her jaw with his thumb. "Had it installed yesterday."

This made her smile widen. She set her hands on his chest and slid them down to rest on his hips. "Just in time for a holiday."

"We'll fire it up later," he said, pressing his lips to her forehead. "What do you say we go for a hike?"

She reeled back. "A hike? Sorry, I only brought these sandals."

"No problem." He grinned, leading her back inside where he opened his closet and handed her a shoebox.

But her gaze was still affixed to the massive walk-in closet, big enough to park a car. Hell, it was bigger than her kitchen in her Queen's apartment.

"Okay, this is another reason I'm in love with this room."

He chuckled and opened the box in her hand. "I guessed your size. Hopefully, they'll fit."

She glanced down at the new hiking boots, which of course, were her exact size. "You know my body well enough to make a great guess."

His gaze heated, but instead of pulling her close, he backed up. "I'll wait for you downstairs."

Sophia stood there, watching him leave, her chest warming with an unknown emotion. It was never more obvious that he wanted to spend time with her, without getting naked. He hadn't brought her here for a booty call. That realization excited and scared her at the same time.

And as the day turned to evening, and they still hadn't exchanged more than several heated embraces, she was empowered by the knowledge that he cared about her beyond the bedroom. Although, she was also…extremely turned on.

Dammit.

Enjoying the glass of wine she'd had with the steak he'd grilled, she sat back on the deck and wiggled her now-bare feet. "That was delicious, Ryder."

He chuckled. "Surprised I can cook?"

"Surprised you knew there was other food besides pizza."

He pointed at her with his beer bottle. "I discovered that hard truth when I started working at my dad's diner after school."

"Ah." She nodded. "I was roped into the family business as a teen, too."

He quirked a brow. "What kind of business is your family into?"

"Construction," she replied, setting her wine on the table. "I still work there full-time and do set design on the side. When Phoebe called to ask me to help her out this summer, it was a godsend. I needed the break."

Not just from work, though. From her mother's never-ending parade of possible fiancé's...and Gino. Yeah, she needed a break from them, too, but he didn't need to know all that.

"You don't do set design full-time?" he asked, surprise tipping his head.

"No. I'd like to, but..." She sighed, not really wanting to talk about it.

He frowned, and something dark passed through his eyes. "But, what, Sophia? Doesn't your family support your work? I mean, they must've to let you go to design school, right?"

She shrugged. "I think they let me enroll so I'd bring my design skills to the family business. And I like it. I do."

"But your heart lies in set design."

She lifted her gaze to his, shocked at how well he knew her. "Yes."

"Then do it," he urged. "If there's one thing I've learned, it's that you can't please everyone."

"I know." She nodded, her stomach flopping at the pain she detected in his tone. "I have a possible shot at set design for a major Broadway show," she confessed. "I have a meeting lined up with them this fall. If I get the job, then my family will hopefully see I can make a living from it."

He didn't laugh or tell her it was foolish. Or a pipedream. Instead, he smiled.

"That's amazing." Nothing but admiration and support filled his gaze as he raised his bottle for a toast. "Here's to you nailing it."

Grabbing her glass, she clinked it against his bottle. "Amen."

Now, more than ever, she was vibrating with need for the man. And since she also wanted to lighten the mood, she set her glass on the table and stood.

"So, tell me, Ryder." She pulled off her dress and removed the tie from her hair. "If I have my way with you in your boat, what would that be considered? The mile...*water* club?"

A flash of heat entered his eyes. "Not sure. But I know it would be great."

"Maybe we should try it." Laughing, she held his gaze as she walked backward to the end of the deck where she quickly stripped out of her bikini.

After kicking off his sneakers, he rose and began to pull off his clothes as he stalked her. "We're going to try a lot of things."

His voice was gruff, and that, combined with his words, sent a shock of heat through her system.

"Last one in the lake takes bottom," she said, before taking off for the dock.

He could've easily overtaken her. Sophia knew this, and didn't care, because top or bottom, either were the best place to be with Ryder.

She could hear him behind her, but he wasn't even trying to beat her to the water.

"You don't need to run," he told her. "In fact, you should go slow. Yeah, real slow."

Laughing, she turned around, watching him approach with desire evident in his dark eyes, and an erection jutting out, leading the way. Her whole body tightened at the sight of his magnificence, then pulsed as he held up a foil packet, opened the boathouse door, and tossed the condom inside.

He was such a boy scout. She loved that about him.

Still holding his gaze, she backed up the last few feet to the edge of the dock, with a deliberate bounce in her steps. "How's that? Better?"

"Mmm…" His eyes smoldered as he stepped closer. "That's delectable."

"Then come get some," she said, stepping off the dock.

The shock of the water stole her breath. It was ninety degrees out and humid. She hadn't expected the lake to be so cold. But she wasn't cold for long. Ryder surfaced with her, pulling her close, electrifying all her nerve-endings where their bodies touched.

He tread water with one hand, and cupped her ass with the other. "Now…about that club."

Chapter Thirteen

Later the following week, Ryder was helping Sophia assemble the burger joint set for Grease, and thinking about their Fourth of July together. It was another holiday they'd spent practically naked, but this time, it was different. This time, it was better. It was more.

More intense.

More amazing.

More everything.

She'd rocked more than the boat, she'd rocked his world. Sharing his space with her, his refuge, had changed things. He discovered he wanted her there. He liked her there. Since then, they spent equal time at each other's place.

And tonight, after they finished working, he planned to take Sophia back to his house.

He wanted her in his bed.

That normally would've had him running the hell away from the woman, but he liked being with her. He liked who he was with her, and he got the impression she felt the same.

So, Ryder decided to loosen his hold on the idea he wasn't good enough for her, because regardless if it was true, she wanted him, flaws and all. She told him, used those very words, not long after she'd straddled him in the hot tub on the Fourth of July, and the fireworks had ceased, both in the sky, and behind his eyes.

Her admission hadn't been fueled by desire, or euphoric fog. She'd meant it, and he believed her. And damn, he wasn't opposed to another round of her in that hot tub. The image of her taking pleasure on him was forever seared into his brain. The way she bucked, panting, fingers digging into his arms, breasts bouncing, gaze dark and smoldering—one eye a dark brown, the other a deep navy. He loved that she'd stopped wearing contacts and liked to think his encouragement to do so helped. Whatever the reason, he was thrilled to stare into her actual eyes, especially when they were full of heat as she cried out his name while he was buried deep inside her.

Ah, hell.

Now he was harder than the damn two-by-fours he'd just screwed together...in a room full of college students.

None of the kids helping out this summer needed much instruction. They were pretty self-sufficient, and for the most part, he was comfortable enough to let them tackle the set jobs on their own. But always happy to answer questions or lend a hand when asked.

Like the young man who'd asked Ryder for help with the Miter saw. Standing back, he watched as the boy measured the three pieces of molding that needed to be cut to frame a doorway. With the door measurement in mind, he had the boy lay the two long pieces parallel to each other on the floor, then measure, mark, and cut the top piece to fit over them.

"Good, now measure and mark where they intersect," he told the boy.

Once that was done, he had him cut off the excess at an angle, then set all three pieces out on the floor again to test the fit.

"Perfect." Ryder cupped the kid's shoulder. "See? Not as hard you as you thought."

The boy smiled, pride straightening his shoulders. "You're right. Thanks."

He watched the boy nail the molding in place around the fake door in the fake wall two other students were starting to paint.

Next, the two of them tackled the red counter for the diner. "This is much easier. No angles. Just a rectangle frame of two-by-fours," he told the boy.

Within ten minutes, they had the frame screwed together, and secured to the top of the makeshift counter.

Once again, Ryder stood back and let the boy take over, watching as he applied the glue to the top of the frame. Then, together they carefully set the pre-cut laminate in place.

"Had this been an actual counter, it would've required a ¾ inch thick piece of cabinet grade birch or oak piece of plywood," he pointed out. "Do you know why we didn't do that?"

The kid nodded. "That would be too heavy for a set that needs to roll on and off the stage."

"Exactly." Ryder slapped the counter and smiled. "Looks great."

"Thanks." The student smiled. "Are we done for the day?"

Sophia approached with a grin. "Yes. Thanks so much for your help. This looks amazing."

Color rushed into the boy's face as he stared at her. Ryder couldn't blame the kid for being flustered. The woman didn't realize how damn beautiful she was, or how sexy.

Today, she had on a white, lacy dress, and he marveled over the fact she managed to work on the set without getting it dirty.

When the boy disappeared off the stage, she stepped closer to him, a wicked gleam entering her eyes. "No one screws better than you," she said, low enough for only his ears.

A certain favorite body part heard and perked up at the praise. "Yeah?"

She grinned. "Yeah. Are you almost ready to go?"

"Almost," he replied, putting away his drill and the rest of his tools in record time. "Now I'm ready."

"Good." She nodded toward the crew. "As soon as they clean up and leave, we can head out, too."

While waiting, Ryder pulled out his phone to check for missed calls. One. The office. Since there were no voicemails, he hit call, hoping to catch Cathy before she left for the day. "Hey, Cathy, what's up?"

"Hi, boss. Sorry to bug you, but you told me to call whenever I got news on a bid."

Something in her tone made him stiffen. "And?"

A sigh rustled through the phone. "We didn't get the ice cream place."

"Are you kidding me?" He swallowed down a curse. "The ice cream parlor? Who got it? Don't tell me Colarusso outbid us again?"

111

Sophia's head snapped in his direction, so he forced himself to calm down. This wasn't the time or place to lose his shit.

"Okay," Cathy said. "I won't tell you, but it was. Sorry. I hope you'll forget about it tonight and enjoy yourself."

Just when he thought he was gaining some ground, out of the blue, Colarusso snagged a job out from under him. He had no fucking clue how they got this one.

Even though the job was on the outskirts of the county, he'd gone low. So low, he'd practically be doing it for free. But the location was sweet, so was the visibility for the company.

Or, at least it would've been if he'd gotten the damn job.

Sophia touched his arm. "I'll be back. I need to go make sure I turned off my computer."

He nodded and watched as she walked off the stage. His chest tightened. He hoped she wasn't put off by his aggravation.

"Did you hear me, Ryder?" Cathy asked. "Go home and enjoy yourself. You still have a few other bids out there."

He blinked, having momentarily forgotten he was still on the phone. "True." He blew out a breath, releasing what was left of his frustration. "I'll see you tomorrow."

"Not too early," Cathy said. "I mean it. Enjoy yourself."

A smile tugged his lips as he hung up the phone. She was right. He wasn't going to let some sleezeball conglomerate ruin his evening, too.

Tonight, was about Sophia, not Colarusso Construction.

***

Happy to find the design room empty, Sophia closed the door behind her and pulled out her phone. Three missed calls—all from Gino—along with three voicemails. Deleting them without even bothering to listen, she breathed an inner sigh of relief that she wasn't in the city to put up with him showing up at her door uninvited.

Everything inside Sophia had frozen when Ryder mentioned her family's company. God, where they really the ones underbidding him all this time?

Her grandmother's maiden name was Colarusso, and it was her grandmother's father—Sophia's great grandfather—who'd started the construction company several generations ago.

When Sophia's father was a teenager, he'd started working there before he and her mother were married. After her grandfather had passed, her dad became the CEO.

Her stomach clenched. How in the world was she ever going to tell any of that to Ryder? Sure, he was a reasonable man, but would he still want to see her? Would he still give them a chance, even though the conglomerate encroaching on his business—possibly causing him to lay off his workers—was her family?

He only just recently opened up. Took her to his house. Let her in a little. Things were still fragile. If he found out, he'd might possibly use her heritage as an excuse the close up again.

113

She didn't want to give him that excuse. Didn't want him to shut her out. She didn't want to lie to him, either.

Dammit.

Everything was screwed up. But, she knew, no matter the outcome, she had to do something to help Ryder. To fix the mess her family made for him and his business.

She swiped the screen, selected favorites, then hit call.

"Colarusso Construction." Her father sounded tired.

"Dad? What are you doing answering the company phones?"

"Sophia! Hi!" His tone brightened. "When are you coming back? We haven't found a good replacement for Mandy, and your mother refuses to help."

Despite the anxiety crushing her chest, she smiled at the idea of her mother sitting behind a desk answering phones.

"I'm desperate. I need your help, Sophia," her father said.

She straightened her shoulders. "Sorry, Dad. I won't be finished here until the end of the summer. I was calling to ask who is in charge of the jobs in the Poconos?"

"Poconos? No one is in Pennsylvania," her dad said.

Someone had to be. She blew out a breath, keeping an eye on the door. "Who's in charge in southwestern New York?"

"Tony? Why?"

"Just wondering," she replied. "Thanks, Dad. Got to go." She hung up and quickly called her brother.

Tony answered on the second ring. "Yo. Sophia, what's up? How's things at the theater?"

"Hi, Tony. Things are good." Or at least, she hoped they would be by the time she got off the phone. "I'm actually calling to ask you to back out of the bid you just won tonight."

He was silent a moment. "What bid?"

"An ice cream parlor," she replied, hating what she was about to do. "I need you to call them back and cancel."

"Sophia." His tone was borderline scolding. "First of all, that's not good business."

She stopped pacing and scowled. "I don't care. You're supposed to be working in New York. Why are you dipping down in Pennsylvania?"

Of course, she knew they had the proper licenses, because she'd been in the office when they'd arrived in the spring.

"Are you telling me Colarusso bid on an ice cream parlor in Pennsylvania?"

She frowned. "Yes."

Tony muttered a curse. "I'll take care of it."

It was weird. Kind of sounded like her brother had no clue.

"Now?"

"Yes, now. Bye, Sophia." He hung up.

She slipped her phone into her back pocket and hadn't even come close to digesting what just happened when a knock sounded at the door. "Yeah?"

Ryder walked in. "Everything okay?"

"Yeah." She smiled, secure in the knowledge that when Tony Nardovino said he was going to do something, he did it. So, Ryder should definitely get that ice cream parlor job. "Is everyone gone?"

"Yep." He stepped close to brush her cheek with his knuckles. "Sure you're okay? I'm sorry about that call. I got angry. I didn't mean to—"

"It's okay," she said, covering his hand on her face with her own. "No need to apologize. Honest." She used her free hand to palm his chest. "So, are you ready to go?"

He dipped down to kiss her softly on the lips. "Now I'm ready."

"Good." She patted his chest. "Because I have a special project we can work on at your place. Are you game?"

Need flickered in his eyes. "I'm all in."

God, she hoped so. Because he hadn't sounded playful. No. He'd sounded serious, like he was talking about them—as a couple, an actual relationship—not just no-strings-attached sex.

Butterflies were still fluttering in her stomach on the drive to his house. He didn't have the truck today. Instead, he drove a gorgeous sports car. The confines were closer. Intimate. It was strange, but she swore she could almost feel him breathing.

"I'd like to show you something," he said, and turned onto a long, secluded, dirt road that dead-ended near a cliff. "I come out here to think sometimes." He cut the engine and faced her. "Thought maybe you might like it."

Like it? "I love it," she said, and got out to lean against the car and look out over the whole valley. "This is breathtaking." It was as if they were nearly as high as the clouds.

For several minutes, she stood next to him, leaning against the car, gazing at the view as the sun slowly started to set. Peace settled over her. A contentment too strong to name. She did her best to catalog the feeling, in order to draw on it when life was less than harmonious.

Which, okay, could be every day. Unless she was with Ryder. He was her anchor. Even when he took her out of herself. He was always there, right beside her.

She turned to him and placed her hand on his thigh. "Thanks for bringing me here. I'll never forget it."

He had one hand on the hood of the car, and the other on his leg, as he leaned in to lightly brush his lips to hers. It was the briefest of connections, and yet, by far the strongest they'd ever shared. Heat skittered through her body, spreading out both north and south, zinging straight to her core.

"Ryder..." she breathed, scared by the depth of emotion and excited at the same time.

He lifted a hand to skim his finger down her cheek. "I know," he said, lips brushing hers as he spoke.

Then he was kissing her again, longer, deeper, and the current intensified, steeling her breath while he zapped her strength. No one kissed like Ryder. It was like heaven on earth.

Donna Michaels

When they drew apart for air, he kissed her forehead, her nose, his mouth hovering above her. "I want you, Sophia."

A tremor shook through her body. "I want you, too, Ryder."

He brushed his lips over hers briefly again. "Let's go."

With a hand on the small of her back, he helped her into the car, before climbing into the driver's seat. After they began to head down the road, he set his hand on her leg, his thumb brushing her knee as if he needed the connection. Needed to touch her.

They didn't say a word on the drive to his house. Didn't need to, because as Elle had once pointed out, their bodies spoke their own language.

Once inside his house, he bent slightly and swept her off her feet.

She looped her arms around his neck and leaned in to kiss his throat. He sucked in a breath, and his hold tightened, and when he entered the master bedroom, he let her slowly slide down his body.

Chapter Fourteen

Something was different.

Something changed. In a good way. Gone was Ryder's indifference. All of it. His barriers. He wasn't holding anything back, and Sophia trembled at the significance of it all.

He was letting her in. She wasn't even sure if he realized it. But, God, what a gift. And she was determined to reward him in kind.

Running her hands up his body, she thrust them into his hair and slowly drew his mouth down to hers, tasting his lips with lazy, lingering passes. This elicited a groan from him. His hands slid down her sides to grip her hips and draw her close as he took over the kiss, devouring her strength with amazing speed.

She released his head to work the buttons on his shirt, brushing his hot skin with her thumb, paying special attention to his abs, loving how he quivered under her touch. He didn't keep still either. His hands skimmed up her back, where his fingers brushed her neck and spine as he slowly tugged her zipper down.

Needing to free his incredible expanse of muscles and ridges, she pushed at his shirt in an attempt to remove it, but her fingers trembled too much to be effective. Hell, her whole body trembled.

He broke the kiss and sucked in air. "I'll get it," he said, voice gruff as he shrugged out of his shirt.

Damn, she was a lucky woman.

Her mouth watered, and her shaky hands itched to explore his hard ridges. But first, she stepped back, letting her loosened dress slip to the floor, leaving her in her sling-back sandals, and pale blue lacy bra and panties.

He sucked in a ragged breath. "God, Sophia. Look at you."

The intense longing in his eyes made her physically ache, and her nipples hardened behind the lace. Wanting to give him more—give him everything—she stepped out of her dress and reached behind her to unhook her bra.

"No." He shook his head and moved closer. "Let me."

Heat from his body washed into her as he hooked his fingers under her bra straps and slowly pulled them down her arms until she sprang free. "Perfect. So perfect." He dipped down to kiss the curve of her breast, and flicked his tongue over her nipple before sucking it hard into his mouth.

Moaning, she closed her eyes and arched into him, feeling his tongue rasp over her nipple, while his hands slid to her back and unhooked her bra, releasing her only long enough to let it drop to the floor. An instant later, he has his mouth on her other nipple, sucking on it until she moaned and clutched his arms.

"So soft," he muttered against her skin as he dragged his mouth up her chest, throat, and jaw, his hands making their way up her back and into her hair. "I can't get enough of you."

His voice was so low and sexy, she felt she could come from the sound alone.

"Me, too." Wrapping her arms around his shoulder blades, she pressed against him, lost in the feel of his hard strength as his arms banded around her, and his mouth finally found hers.

He tasted warm and intoxicating, and she loved the ragged groan she wrenched from his chest when she rocked against him. Without breaking the kiss, he lifted her up and set her on the bed, following her down on the mattress.

She felt deliciously naughty in her panties and sandals, while he still wore his jeans and work boots. Deciding to do something about it, while he continued to kiss her slow and deep, zapping her brain cells, she reached between them to unhook his jeans.

When they broke for air, he stared down at her. His eyes were dark and very, very hot.

"Not, yet." He kissed a path along her collarbone and down between her breasts, his tongue taking a detour over her pebbled peak while he ground against her.

Need shot out in all directions. She clutched his arms and arched up, but he moved south, dragging his mouth over her ribs, stopping to swirl his tongue into her belly button. His touch was different. Like he was grounded. Stronger. Sure. He nipped at her hip, then kissed her low on her belly, and air shuddered out of her when he hooked his fingers in her panties and tugged them down her legs, his mouth following in hot pursuit.

"So sweet," he murmured against her ankle as he pulled the lace completely off, then removed her sandals and stood to quickly strip out of the rest of his clothes, and set a condom on the bed.

The sight of him staring down at her, eyes blazing with intense need, made her breath catch. His fingers encircled her ankles and tugged them apart. "You're so damn beautiful."

While she melted, he kissed her shin, her knee, then inner thigh, his broad shoulders nudging her wide. His breath was warm on her sensitized skin as he stopped to look his fill.

"Ryder." She squirmed.

"But…if you could just see…" He bent and kissed an inner thigh, and she thought, *higher*. He was so close. Then he gently stroked her, and she closed her eyes, lost in his touch. He groaned and placed his mouth on her, teasing her with his tongue.

She moaned and fisted his comforter, writhing beneath him, silently urging him to continue.

"I love how you taste," he murmured, cupping her ass cheeks to hold her in place during his ministrations. His attention to detail was a gift, because he was hitting spots she didn't know existed. Quicker than she expected, he had her quivering on the edge.

Then he stopped.

But before she could catch her breath, or complain, he shifted higher, kissing her breast, tugging her nipple into his mouth as his finger unexpectedly stroked her center, then slipped inside.

She cried out, and he sucked in a breath.

"So wet." He lifted his head and stared down at her, his gaze smoldering and intent. Leaning on his elbow, he continued to watch her as he slowly slid his finger all the way out in an upward angle, then back down.

"Mmm...yes," she muttered, arching up.

Doing it again, he slid up in a mind-numbingly long stroke, then down in an equally long stroke, then her added another finger.

"Ryder..." Breath caught in her throat. "Love that..."

As if knowing what she wanted—what she needed—before she did, he upped the pace, building the tension until she was ready to snap.

"Sophia. Look at me," he ordered in a strained, hoarse tone she felt all the way to her throbbing core.

She managed to open her eyes halfway. "Don't stop."

He didn't. The intuitive man brushed his thumb over her center between strokes and that sent her spiraling over the edge.

Crying out his name, she gripped his wrists and bucked into his touch, all while holding his gaze. When she slowed her hips, he slowed his strokes, prolonging her orgasm until she was spent.

When he released her, he bent down to kiss her lips, his gaze still glued to hers. Satisfaction and heat blazed in his blue depths, increasing the quivering in her belly. "That was amazing."

"No, you were amazing," she said, kissing him harder. Deeper. Never wanting to let him go.

***

Ryder was ready to burst.

The amazing woman...*his* amazing woman was hot and willing, and writhing beneath him. If she kept that up, he wasn't going to last. Groaning, he broke the kiss. "Hold that thought."

Reaching for the foil packet, he used the time to get his breathing under control. And his body. He wanted to savor the incredible feel of being inside her, not lose it like some damn teenager.

He removed the condom and was rolling it on when her hand joined in and he swore she was trying to make him lose his mind. Her lingering strokes were exquisite, but he wasn't that strong.

In fact, he was putty in her hands, and proved it when he rocked into her touch, as if he had no control.

Because he fucking didn't.

Not with her.

Chapter Fifteen

"I need you, Ryder." She guided him to the promised land, and gazed up at him with a fierce hunger that darkened her eyes to that deep chocolate and navy that he loved so much.

Needing no other prompting, he settled between her legs, but didn't push inside. Not yet. He entwined their fingers and lifted their joined hands to rest on either side of her face.

"I need you inside me," she whispered, her voice sexy and hoarse with need.

He dipped down to softly kiss her lips. "I need that too."

He needed everything. Wanted everything. And wanted to give her everything, too.

With one last kiss, he held her gaze and slid into her. Home. That's what she was to him. Everything. His world. She cried out his name, and it mixed with his groan, echoing the sound of their mutual pleasure.

"God, Sophia…" He closed his eyes, basking in the feel of her lush heat. "You feel so—always so damn good." The way he filled her—the way she hugged him—it rocked him to his very soul.

"Ryder," she whispered on a hitched breath.

He loved how her head arched back and lips parted. Unable to resist, he bent down and captured her open mouth with his, slipping his tongue inside, thrilling at the sound of her moan. Her tongue brushed his as she rocked her hips, doing her damnedest to make him cross-eyed.

Breaking the kiss, he lifted up to stare into her eyes, needing to see she was just as thrown, as lost...as found, as he was in the crazy rush of heat, and need, and want. She wrapped her legs around him and arched up, and he felt himself slipping further inside.

And further in love.

Yeah, he loved her. She did it for him. Understood his moods. His needs. She was open, honest, held nothing back. He loved that about her, too. She got him. She understood and accepted. And, God, that was such a heady feeling.

He could tell she was falling for him, too. It was in her sighs, her kisses, the tender way she sometimes touched his face. The way her face lit up when he walked into the room. It used to scare him, now...it strengthened him.

But right now, the feel of her soft curves trembling beneath him, the way her breasts brushed his chest, how she hugged him tight inside, was all too much. She was too much. He had no strength left. He needed to start moving, to take them to the next level.

"Sophia," he whispered hoarsely, squeezing their entwined fingers, as he began to move.

A low, sexy sound rumbled in her chest, and she matched his rhythm, apparently lost in the same delirious need consuming him from the inside out.

"Ryder..." Her gaze was open and full of all the emotions he was feeling in her touch.

"I know," he murmured, letting her see exactly what she did to him, exactly how he felt about her.

He was done talking, he could only feel. Lost in the wave of heat, he locked his elbows, and upped their pace. Damn, she felt good. Her low moans and the way she arched into him stole his breath, and captured his heart.

Freeing her hands from his, she shoved them in his hair, like she needed to hold onto him, needed him to ground her.

And he knew then. Ryder knew that *this* was what it felt like when it was right.

He slid his arms beneath her and gripped her shoulders from behind. The movement brought them closer, and he slid deeper inside. She cried out and whispered his name over and over as she shuddered and quivered against him in the most amazing, fucking climax that spurred his own fierce release.

Later, after he found his bones and cleaned up, he climbed under the covers with her, and knew everything had changed. His outlook had changed. He'd changed. He wanted her in his life full-time and was willing to commute, or anything else she wanted to make that happen.

The soft, sweet woman in his arms had a little over five weeks left before she headed back to New York. He was determined to use that time to help her realize she was happiest with him. God knew, he was with her.

Euphoric exhaustion set in, and he fell asleep to the soft sounds of her breathing, knowing he didn't ever want to let her go.

***

Sophia hated keeping things from Ryder.

Especially after everything they shared last night, and again that morning before they got dressed and headed into town to work.

As much as she wanted to spend the day in his bed, surrendering herself to a multitude of mind-blowing orgasms, she needed to finish the set of the car so tomorrow she could start on the beauty shop. Besides, he told her he had a kitchen remodel he needed to finish by Friday.

That meant no surrendering or mind-blowing orgasms until tonight, after dinner at a restaurant he told her had a view almost as amazing as the one he shared with her yesterday.

Maybe then she'd tell him about her family. She'd tried, on several occasions, but each time, he either kissed her senseless, and she forgot what she was going to say, or fear got in the way. The fear of him slipping back into that safe zone of indifference and shutting her out.

He hadn't shut her out this morning, though. A smile tugged her lips. That was why they were running a little late.

"My sister must be here," he said, parking in the parking lot in a spot in front of the theater next to Ben's truck.

She nodded. "Lea was bringing donuts, so we can nibble and chat while I work on the car set. I'm guessing Ben brought her. I think he likes to be with his girls as much as possible."

"I can relate," Ryder said, gaze open and warm, causing her heart to catch. "We still on for dinner tonight?"

Smiling, she opened her mouth to reply when his phone rang.

He lifted it from the cup holder where he'd set it, and sent her an apologetic look. "It's the office. I won't be long."

"No problem," she replied, her pulse tripping while she waited to see if it had to do with the ice cream parlor.

"Hey, Cathy. I'm on my way." He stilled. "What? We did?" His gaze narrowed before pleasure straightened his brow. "That's fantastic news. I wonder what happened to make Colarusso back out?"

Sophia knew, and relief helped her breath in some air, while making a mental note to thank her brother.

"I will. Thanks. See you in a few minutes," he said, before hanging up. "I don't believe it." A slight smile curved his lips while bewilderment rounded his gaze. "Colarusso backed out. I got the ice cream parlor job."

"That is fantastic news," she said, heart hammering out of control.

This was it. The perfect time to come clean. To tell him about her family, and how she'd asked them to back off and they did. Her family was not

129

unreasonable. They weren't the enemy. Neither was she. He'd see that. Surely, he would.

Her palms were sweaty, and they shook, so she entwined her fingers to keep them steady on her lap.

"Guess the New York big shots bit off more than they could handle. Spread themselves too thin." He shook his head and frowned. "And put honest, hardworking people like me out of business."

The need to defend her family because too much. "They probably started out the same way."

His brow rose, then he shrugged. "Maybe, but it's companies like that that tick me off."

And everything she was about to get off her chest died on her lips. Maybe it would be better when he wasn't so worked up.

"Sorry," he said, reaching out to play with a strand of her hair. "Let's get back to my question." Leaning close, he dragged his mouth across her jaw to her ear where he nibbled.

His question, her family, their jobs, how to breathe...everything disappeared into the warm, sensuous fog taking over her mind.

"Mmm..." She fisted his shirt and tipped her head to give him better access. "I like the way you ask."

He chuckled near her ear. "I like the way you taste."

She turned her head to give him her mouth when her phone started to ring. Setting her forehead to his jaw, she sighed. "Think we should've stayed in bed."

"We can always go back." Amusement and heat were evident in his tone.

Her body perked up at the suggestion, but she fished out her phone and did her best to ignore the awareness pooling low in her belly. She glanced at the screen, and frowned. "It's my dad." She answered as Ryder shifted back to his seat, "What's wrong?"

"How do you women do that?" he said. "It's like a sixth sense or something. I'm calling because you need to come home."

She swallowed a groan. "If this is about answering phones, I—"

"No," he cut her off. "It's about your mother. She's at the hospital in the emergency room."

Chapter Sixteen

Sophia's heart dropped to her knees. "What's wrong?"

A warm hand covered hers and squeezed. She glanced at Ryder, finding the warmth and concern in his eyes a welcomed comfort.

"She has stomach pains. Apparently, she's had them for days and hasn't said anything. I married a stubborn woman." Her father huffed. "I told her to go easy on the pepperoncini, but does she listen? No. Now they want to admit her to take out her gallbladder."

Gallbladder?

Okay, she breathed a little easier. That was kind of routine.

"She keeps going on about a night coat or house shirt, or something," her father continued in a frustrated rush. "I don't know what she's talking about. I need you back here to help me get what she wants, and to help her when she's home recovering. I won't be able to stay home. I'll need to get back to work. And you know how willful she gets. I can't trust her to not overdo it. Someone has to watch her."

"It's okay," she rushed to say, already mentally going over the set schedule in her mind. "I'll leave in a few minutes and drive straight to your house to grab what Ma needs." She glanced at the clock on the dashboard. "I should be at the hospital by two. What time is her surgery?"

"Don't know yet." He sighed. "I'll call you when I do."

"Okay. I'll see you soon," she said before hanging up.

Ryder gently squeezed her hand, regaining her attention. "You okay?"

She nodded, feeling exhausted and full of adrenaline at the same time. "I have to go home. Well, to my parents', then the hospital. My mother needs—"

"Her gallbladder out," he finished for her, slight smile on his lips. "I heard."

A snort escaped her. "Yeah…my family's kind of loud."

Understatement of the year.

"What can I do?" He brought her hand to his lips and kissed her knuckles.

Her chest warmed, and everything inside her softened. "You're doing it. Thanks. And I'm sorry. I'll be gone a few weeks. I'll need to be there while my mom recovers. Family comes first, right?" She smiled, but he didn't return it. Not even a flicker.

As if realizing she was waiting for his reply, he nodded. "Right."

But she got a weird vibe, like maybe he hadn't quite been there. That he was lost in the past. A bad one.

Trepidation skittered down her spine. She brushed it off. It was just shock from the unexpected call, she told herself.

"What about Phoebe, and the youth show?" he asked, releasing her hand.

"It'll be okay. I'm sure she'll understand," she said. "We've already got some of the sets built. And all the instructions are done. I know you and the others will do an amazing job." A technical director is usually the one who oversaw the construction, anyway. It wasn't usually the set designer, but Sophia didn't bother to explain since she was doubling as both for Phoebe. "I trust you to take over…if that's okay?"

He nodded, but his mind seemed far away.

Reaching over, she cupped his chin and leaned close. "Thanks," she said against his lips. "I'm going to miss you." It took all her control to keep from blurting out that she loved him. The timing was wrong. She couldn't just say it and then leave.

But she could show him. And did, pressing her mouth to his.

After hesitating long enough for her heart to stop and rock, he finally slid his hands into her hair and returned the kiss. Once the tightness in her chest eased, she relaxed against him. But all too soon, he broke the kiss and set his forehead to hers.

"I'm going to miss you, too," he said, running a finger from her temple to her jaw.

And as she left him to go inside the theater in search of Phoebe, Sophia's chest tightened once more.

What if he closed up again? She didn't think she could bear it if he shut her out now. It wasn't just sex anymore. It wasn't just a good time. Not for her, and not for him. She knew it, felt it.

She just hoped it was still there when she came back.

***

Ten days without Sophia might as well have been two lifetimes. Ryder was shocked to realize how much he'd grown accustomed to having the woman in his life. He missed her smiles, and laughter, her teasing, and taste, her sexy cries, and soft curves.

He was an idiot. He should've told her he loved her before she'd left. It would've given her a reason to come back, in case their great sex wasn't enough.

Christ, he missed hot sex with her.

"Hey, buddy." Ben dropped into the booth across from him, bringing his mind back to the fact he was in his dad's restaurant, stirring sugar in an empty mug. "You may want to add some coffee to that."

He snickered, reaching for the carafe in the middle of the table. "Definitely need caffeine."

Ben chuckled. "That's not all you need. It's Sophia you're lacking, not coffee."

He blew out a breath and nodded, filling his mug. No sense in denying it. His buddy was too astute, and a really good bullshit detector.

"She still in the city helping her mother?" Ben turned his mug over and emptied the carafe.

"Yeah." He nodded. "Probably for another week."

He wasn't going to last. The withdrawals were murder. His chest fucking ached. What was up with that?

"Jammed at work?"

Not as much as he'd like to be, but he hadn't lost any of his recent bids. "No more than usual."

Right now, he had three remodels going on. Two residential, the other commercial. And on Monday, he was scheduled to break ground on the ice cream parlor.

It was the free time at night that was killing him.

"How about the theater?" Ben asked, pushing the carafe to the end of the table with the lid up to let Elle know it was empty.

"Finished up the last set last night." He hoped they did Sophia's designs justice. Phoebe seemed pleased, so he had to assume they'd hit the mark.

In less than thirty seconds, Elle dropped off a full carafe, and removed the empty. "The usual today, guys?"

They both nodded.

"How's Sophia's mom?" she asked.

"Good," he replied. Driving her crazy, from what she'd told him last night on the phone. His lips twitched because there might've been a more colorful version involving bats and shit. "Her follow up doctor's appointment is tomorrow, I believe."

Ben smiled. "That's good. Maybe she'll be back sooner than expected and cure your lonely-ass blues."

Idiot.

"She has a big family, right?" Elle asked.

"Yeah."

"So, it's safe to bet there are others around in the evening?"

He frowned, too clueless to see where this was all leading.

Ben snorted. "You're going to have to spell out whatever it is you're getting at, Elle. Neither of us have had enough coffee in our system to decode women's logic."

"Not sure it has anything to do with coffee," she said dryly, meeting his gaze. "Okay, bottom line, Sophia can't come here because she's taking care of her mom. Why can't you go there?"

He stilled, his mind reeling at something so obvious, yet he'd been oblivious. "Visit her?"

Elle nodded. "Yes. If she has a big family, I'm sure someone could sit with her mother while she goes out on a date with you." Winking, she slapped his shoulder with her order pad, then headed toward the kitchen. "I'll be back with your food in a bit."

His gaze met Ben's.

"Yeah. Never would've thought of that," his buddy said, shaking his head. "But don't tell your sister. I'm starting to get a reputation for being sensitive to her needs, and I don't need to disillusion her."

Ryder's stomach instantly clenched. "Ah, hell. Did you have to go there?"

"What?" His buddy reeled back. "I wasn't talking about *those* needs...although..."

"Don't even think it." He held up his hand and glared.

Ben chuckled. "So...what time you leaving for the city?"

He sat back in the booth as excitement rushed through him for the first time in days. "As soon as Sophia tells me. I'll have to get her parents' address, too." No sooner had the words left his mouth when his phone vibrated on the table with her caller ID on the screen. He grinned. "Hi, Ben and I were just talking about you."

"Good things, I hope." Her tone was light with amusement.

"Of course," he replied. "I was just telling him I need to get your parents' address, so I can maybe come to see you."

There was a slight pause, and his excitement nosedived.

Chapter Seventeen

"Aww, that's sweet," Sophia said, sounding pleased, which went a long way to resurrecting his calm. "But I can do you one better. It's actually why I'm calling."

"Oh?" Ryder's pulse increased, proving that excitement hadn't completely died out.

"Any chance you can get away later to catch a Mets game with me?"

Keiffer's townhouse and the game they'd watched together immediately sprang to mind. They'd only caught five innings, but it'd turned out to be the best damn game...certainly the most memorable. "I'd love to watch a game with you again."

That seventh inning stretch had rocked his world.

"Mmm...I'd love that, too. But, I'm actually talking about seeing the game in person, not on television."

He sat up straight, anticipation thrumming through his veins. "At the stadium?"

Ben's head snapped up, envy gleaming in his gaze.

"Yes." She laughed. "You game?"

He couldn't stop the grin from spreading across his face. "What time should I meet you? And where?"

"Hmm…" Her tone was playful. "I get the feeling you're more excited about the game than seeing me."

"Not true." He snickered. "I'm equally excited about both."

Her soft chuckle sent shivers down his spine. "I'll take it. And you."

He wanted to tell her she could have him, but his buddy was way too close for him to get into a private conversation with her. "Deal," he said instead.

"Perfect. I'll text you the address to my apartment. It's closer to the stadium, so I'll meet you there, say around five-thirty? If that's okay. This way my dad will be home from work to take care of my mom, and you and I can…get something to eat first."

Her slight hesitation wasn't lost on him or his body. It immediately picked up on her unspoken innuendo, and the horny bastard tightened with unchecked gusto.

"Deal," he repeated, shifting to relieve the pressure behind his zipper.

"I'll see you then," she said, before hanging up, and a few seconds later, a text came in with her address.

Ever since she'd left, he'd fought an inner battle. Scars of desertion, of family coming first, of not being enough, they all tormented his mind. Deep down, he knew this was different. That Sophia wasn't Jinan, and yet, old hurts resurfaced, causing doubts, and unwarranted pain. And guilt. He felt bad—

140

selfish—for not wanting her to leave him to take care of her sick mother.

Just because he felt guilty about it didn't make him any less of a dick.

Feeling his buddy's gaze on him, he glanced up. "What?"

Ben smirked. "Don't count on seeing the game tonight, man. You're going to be otherwise occupied."

A smile spread across his face as world-rocking memories crowded his mind.

In the grand scheme of things, Ryder was okay with that.

***

"Why are you all smiles today?" her mother asked.

Sophia stopped straightening the stack of magazines on the coffee table and glanced at her mother, convalescing on the couch. "I wasn't aware I was smiling."

What she had been doing was thinking about Ryder and the fact she would see him in less than an hour.

"You've got a dreamy look in your eyes, too. And I noticed you're not wearing your contacts. You're not covering up the real you. It's about time." Her mother grinned. "So, who is he?"

She snickered and shook her head, ready to give a vague answer when her mother spoke again.

"Is it that Ryder guy?"

Sophia's heart rocked clear up into her throat. "How...?"

Her mother chuckled. "I know things. I also took a train to see your sets for Oklahoma."

"You did? When?" She sank onto the loveseat and stared across at the smiling sneakpot. "Why didn't you come find me?"

"It was opening weekend. I got there just as the curtain went up, so there was no time to find you before the show. And when I went to find you afterward, you were in the arms of a very handsome man. A very nice lady told me his name. I've never seen you so happy." Tears glistened in her mother's eyes. "Are you still seeing him?"

She nodded, unable to keep the smile from her face. "He's great. He makes me feel…amazing."

"I noticed you have *the passion*. That is good. I witnessed it firsthand." Her mother fanned herself.

Heat rushed into Sophia's face. "Ma—"

"What?" Her mother frowned. "I was young once. I remember *the passion*. Your father and I still have it, we're just not as spontaneous as in our youth."

And Sophia really didn't need to know any more. "Okay. I get it."

Her mother chuckled. "You'll be my age someday, just wait. And with the right person, hopefully, you'll be just as happy."

Her parents always had a loving relationship, it's the reason Sophia never settled for any of the guys paraded at her. None of them made her feel…none of them ever connected. Not like Ryder.

"You love him, don't you?" Her mother's gaze softened.

She nodded, her own insides going mushy. "Yes. I do."

"I thought so." A pleased expression spread across her face. "That's why I haven't called so much. Or mentioned any guys. I was hoping you found a good man on your own. So...what's he like? I already know he's not Italian, but that's okay. I won't hold it against him. Now, your father...I'm not so sure."

With a light heart, Sophia told her mother about Ryder and his family, and some of the less racy moments from her summer with him.

"I'm sorry I pulled you away." Remorse clouded her mother's gaze. "I don't see any reason for you to still hang around here." She brushed imaginary lint off the blanket surrounding her and huffed. "Your father is just too overprotective."

"He loves you, and doesn't want you to overdo it—like you usually do," Sophia said.

"Well, I'm fine now. You can go back."

She chuckled. "Next week. It'll be fourteen days, and that's when the doctor says you're okay to do certain things," she reminded.

"But, your man...you can't keep him waiting."

She smiled. "I've been talking to him every day, and as a matter of fact, he's meeting me in a half hour. We're going to the Mets game tonight."

Her mother's face brightened. "He likes the Mets? See? I knew there was a reason I got a good vibe about him."

Sophia got lots of good vibes, both *about* and *from* the man.

"Your brother's coming in for the game, too," her mother continued. "Maybe you can go together. Is Ryder coming here? I finally get to meet him?"

Her parents lived fifteen minutes from her, so they were both about the same distance to the stadium, but having Ryder meet her here wasn't a good idea. Her father would be home soon, and her brothers would no doubt drop in. All they'd have to do was talk about work and disaster would strike. Definitely not the way she wanted him to find out about the family company.

It had to come from her. And it would.

She'd made up her mind to tell him, but not until she was back at work in the Poconos. This way, if he had an issue and tried to pull back, she would be near to do something about it. If she told him while in New York, there would be too much time and distance between them, and it was possible she'd never be able to bridge that gap.

"No." She shook her head. She couldn't, wouldn't take that chance. "We're meeting at my place. I need to change." She glanced at the clock on the wall. "As soon as Dad gets here."

Of course, today of all days, he had to be late.

When he arrived ten minutes later, she kissed them both on the cheek and took off for home. With luck, she'd get there just before Ryder was due. He'd texted her when he'd gotten through the city. Twenty-eight minutes ago.

Luck, indeed was on her side, though. Traffic was surprisingly light for that time of day, especially on a game night. She lived about five miles from the ballpark and knew things could get hectic.

Snagging one of the few parking spots in front of her building, she got out, stepped onto the sidewalk, then noticed a very familiar, sexy, blue-eyed man leaning against an equally familiar silver car a few spots down.

Sophia's heart leapt. "Ryder." Smiling, she rushed into his open arms, loving the way they banded around her as his mouth found hers.

God, she missed this. Missed his kisses. Missed him.

Uncaring that she was in the middle of the sidewalk and that people had to walk around them, she eagerly gave into *the passion*.

When they finally broke for air, he rested his forehead against hers—a move she really loved—and met her gaze. "Hi." His eyes were dark and heated. "I needed that."

"Me, too." She grinned, running her palms over his shoulders to lock behind his head. "In fact, I think I may need a little more."

"God...me, too," he uttered against her mouth, and kissed her slower, deeper, apparently not caring about the whistles and snickers and sighs going on around them, either.

But the sound of tires screeching and doors slamming had them both breaking apart in time to see her brother and Gino glaring at them, from beside a white van with *Colarusso Construction* printed on the side.

"What the hell?" Ryder's gaze narrowed as he stared at the men and the truck.

Oh, God.

All the air in her lungs gathered to form a tight ball in her chest. This wasn't happening, she thought to herself. Why in the world were her brother and Gino here? Her mind reeled, and her chest squeezed, but she knew none of that was going to help defuse the situation.

"Sophia? Who is this guy?" Tony asked, suspicion darkening his eyes.

"Yeah, Sophia," Gino piped up. "Who is this guy?"

Stiffening, Ryder transferred his attention back to her. "You know them? You know Colarusso?"

"Know them? She *is* them," Gino stated, with a pompous lift to a chin her fist itched to smack.

"Shut up, Gino," her brother muttered, no doubt sensing her distraught state.

Ryder released her and stepped back. "All this time…and you said nothing?" The tiny sliver of light left in his eyes flickered and went out.

Sucking in some much-needed air, she set her hand on his arm. "I can explain."

"I want him to explain why he had his mouth on my fiancée," Gino grumbled from behind.

Pain twisting his face, Ryder yanked free. "Fiancée?"

"No. We're not engaged." She stepped toward him, but he moved away. "Please, let me explain," she said again, her chest crushed so tight she could barely breathe. "Ryder, please."

But his gaze was closed and cold, miles past indifferent. "You had more than enough time for that," he stated in a hard tone, before climbing in his car and driving away without a backward glance.

"You're better off without that pretty boy, anyway," Gino said, taking his life in his hands, because she was damn close to losing it.

Twisting around, she strode straight to him and shook her fist in his face. "Gino, so help me, you better listen and listen good, because I will *not* say this again. I will never marry you. Ever. Leave me the hell alone. We may have grown up together, but I don't like you right now. I really don't."

And if her throat hadn't closed on her, she would've told him to get lost.

"But I've been working my ass off getting jobs this summer, so we can have a big wedding," he said, truly clueless to how close she teetered to the edge.

Tony stepped forward, expression dark, jaw tight as he wedged himself between them. "You heard my sister, she said she doesn't want you. Don't ever harass her again." He slapped the keys to the idiot's chest. "Take the van and get out of here. You can pick me up at my parents' house in the morning."

Something in her brother's tone must've gotten through to the guy's thick head, because he closed his mouth and got in the van.

By this time, her bravado and strength were just about spent. Her whole body shook.

"Come on." Tony slid his arm around her. "Let's get you inside and you can explain to me what the hell just happened."

She snorted. At least, that was what she was going for, but a strangled sound came out instead. "The man I love hates me," she muttered, leaning against him as he helped her inside, and upstairs into her third-floor apartment.

He sat her down on her couch, then disappeared into her kitchen and returned to shove a glass of water in her hands. "Tell me what's going on," he said, sitting next to her.

After sipping some water, she set the glass on her coffee table because her hands were shaking too much. And she was cold. God, she was so cold. Fighting tears, she told him briefly about her relationship with Ryder, and then about how their company was underbidding and hurting his business.

Tony blew out a breath and shoved a hand in his thick, dark hair. Although she loved her middle brother dearly, right now, she wanted to smack him, too.

"Why were you even bidding in Pennsylvania, Tony?" she asked with a shake of her head. "Surely there's still enough work in New York?"

He dropped his hand and twisted to face her. "It wasn't me. Gino's the one who's been doing the bids."

"Gino?"

Tony nodded. "I confronted him after you'd called about that ice cream parlor bid. Turns out he's been dividing his crew in half and working two areas. I put a stop to it. He was overworking his men. I made sure they got paid." He set a hand on her back. "I'm sorry, I didn't know until you'd called. I assumed he was just working the New York jobs I gave him."

Anger fisted tight in her chest as she focused on the company. It was safer than letting her thoughts drift to her mess with Ryder. "Did he at least pay the workers?"

"Yeah. I made sure of it." Tony scowled. "I also went through the material receipts on the jobs he did, and had to go in and replace a few things to make sure the job was up to Colarusso standards. I appreciate the initiative but not the execution."

"What was he thinking?"

"That you were going to marry him, I guess. Although, that'd be over my dead body." He smirked.

She was too raw to respond to that. "Does Dad know about this?"

"Yes." Tony nodded, easily going along with her subject change. "And Gino's on probation. Doesn't matter how good of friends Dad is with his dad, he won't stand for jeopardizing the Colarusso name."

Her control was starting to slip, so she just nodded, and fought through the burning behind her eyes.

A strangled sound rumbled in her brother's throat as he pulled her into his chest. "What can I do to help?"

"Nothing." She sniffed and burrowed closer. "Ryder was right. I should've told him." The damage was done. It was up to her to try and fix things. To explain. And, oh yeah, she was definitely going to track him down and explain. But it would have to wait until she could go back to the Poconos.

She just hoped it wasn't too late.

Hoped it was enough.

Chapter Eighteen

Ryder cracked open a can of beer as he sat at the edge of his dock and stared out at the lake. Still vast. Tranquil. Loaded with fish. Sun still glittered off it without mercy. Nothing about the vista had changed over the past four days.

Unlike him. He hadn't been the same since New York.

Hell, he didn't even really remember driving home the other night. He'd been numb, operating on autopilot. It wasn't until he'd passed a frowning Ben by the armory that his dazed brain had realized he was back in Pennsylvania.

His buddy had signaled for him to stop, but he shook his head and kept driving. No reason to stop. Talking wasn't going to help. And he hadn't been in the mood for any type of company, so he'd gone straight home, parked in the driveway, and stared at his house. A house full of memories of the woman whose betrayal cut so deep it hurt to fucking breathe.

Even now, his chest was too tight to get a full breath into his lungs. But the beer was going down pretty smooth. He sucked down the cold brew and eyed the boathouse.

He hadn't been inside there yet, either. Or his workshop, because he had memories of her in those places too. Didn't leave him with many choices to sleep that first night. So, he'd grabbed a sleeping bag from his shed, and slept in the back of the truck.

For three nights now.

Work was good, though. Busy. A godsend. He'd thrown himself into it, glad his volunteer work was done at the theater. Until the next show. Sophia had one more to design, but screw it. He was going to sit that one out.

Maybe he'd sit on the dock and have a beer then, too.

"You ever going to answer your phone?" Ben asked from behind, his boots clomping on the stairs…along with another set.

Ryder's heart stopped a few beats, as longing—the traitor—trickled through his chest in the hopes it was Sophia. Although, he didn't even know if she was back in town yet.

He turned around to find the oldest Wyne brother approaching too, and told himself it was relief that ricocheted through his gut.

"You didn't toss it in the lake, did you?" Ethan asked.

Ryder smirked. "Thought about it." Even went so far as to grip the damn thing in his hand. It was loaded with texts and missed calls and voicemails from family and friends, but the majority were from Sophia. He didn't want to talk to her. Didn't want to see her. "I shut it off and shoved it in my glove box."

Didn't matter, though. He'd had little peace since then. Not from his mind, anyway.

151

"You didn't show up for our lunch today," Ben said, easing down beside him, before opening the cooler to peek inside. "A liquid diet, huh?"

Ethan sat down on his other side and smirked. "That's nutritious."

"I remember those days." Ben tossed a beer to Ethan, before securing one for himself.

Ryder knew what they were doing, and it wasn't going to work. "Don't get too comfortable. I don't want company, and I'm not in the mood to talk."

"That's okay," Ethan said. "We'll do the talking."

"Yeah." Ben cupped his shoulder and nodded. "We've been friends a long time, and I get where you're coming from, I really do, but I can't let you be. Not now that your sister is involved. She's worried about you, and losing sleep over it." He squeezed his shoulder. "You have to understand, I won't let her suffer. So, it's time for an intervention."

Ryder muttered an oath. Lea wasn't getting a ton of sleep with the baby as it was, he didn't want her losing even more over him. "Tell her I'm fine and not to worry."

"Yeah, you're doing great, all right," Ben scoffed, releasing him. "You have a sleeping bag in the back of your truck, and you're drinking beer for lunch. She'll be thrilled to hear that. I'm sure she'll sleep better than our daughter, now."

He scrubbed a hand over his face and shook his head. "Look, I'm fine. This is the first beer I've had since...all week." He couldn't bring himself to reference that night in the city.

The hiss of air escaping the can pierced the air as Ethan cracked open his beer. "We've been where you are, Ryder. And believe it or not, it only got better when someone pointed out we were acting like asses."

"Okay, so we still act like it sometimes," Ben added. "But, my brother's right. When it came to the women we love, we were blind to our misconceptions. So, chances are, that's what you're dealing with, too. Surely, the three of us can figure it out."

"And if not, Phoebe and Lea are on standby." Ethan nodded, patting the phone visible in his shirt pocket.

"After all, they're the ones who told us what went down in New York."

"How'd they know?" He certainly hadn't told anyone.

"Sophia," Ethan replied. "She's been calling daily, hoping we'd see you and ask you to call her." The guy looked deadpan at him. "Ryder, can you please call Sophia?"

"Not gonna happen." Not in this lifetime. He'd had enough betrayal from women. He was done.

Ethan pursed his lips and nodded. "You could always go see her. She's back in town. Arrived last night."

The news hit him like a blow to the solar plexus. He straightened his spine and drew in a breath. *Did she even try to find him?* He brushed the stupid thought aside. Didn't matter. He wouldn't have spoken to her anyway.

"Okay, then, it's time to hash things out," Ben said, before swigging down some beer.

"Nothing to hash out," he muttered. "She's a Colarusso. Knew about my issues with them and said nothing. Probably had a good laugh, too. Oh, and she's engaged to some guy named Gino, who I suspect was the one putting in the bids. He looked familiar. She was probably telling him about the jobs I was trying to get. She's devious and conniving, and I'm done."

Ben glanced around him at his brother. "Was I that stupid?"

Ethan nodded. "You were worse."

"I think we're done." Gritting his teeth, he made to get up, but each man gripped one of his shoulders and held him in place.

"No. Not hardly, so stay put," Ben said, voice firm and serious, all signs of teasing gone. "First off, she's not engaged and hasn't been. That was some yahoo who won't let her alone."

"What?" Without permission, Ryder's insides knotted and a strong urge to beat the shit of the guy surged through him.

"And she didn't lie about her last name. It's Nardovino. But her family does own Colarusso Construction. It was her grandfather on her mother's side who started the business."

"Whatever," he muttered. "She never told me." She kept secrets. End of story.

Ben quirked a brow. "Did you ask?"

He jerked his head back. "What?"

"Did you ask her if she was a Colarusso?"

"Of course not." Ryder finished his beer then squeezed the empty can in his hand. Fucking idiot.

His buddy cocked his head. "Then explain exactly how it is she lied."

"By omission."

Ben smirked. "That's thin, man."

"Real thin." Ethan nodded.

"See through," Ben continued, doing a great job of pissing him off, too.

Ryder opened the cooler and tossed the crushed can inside, before grabbing a new one. "This has been fun. Not," he said. "Are you two going to come to a point soon? I need to finish drinking alone."

Ben inhaled, then spoke, "From what I gathered from your remarks, you think Sophia used you to get the locations of the jobs you wanted to bid on, so she could pass it on to some stalker that works for her family, so her family could bid lower and get the jobs. Am I right?"

"No. Yeah...Christ." He blew out a breath. "I don't know." His brain hurt. When he heard it out loud, it sounded stupid. "She lied to me."

Ethan shook his head. "No, Ryder, she just didn't tell you everything, and it's my guess that she was worried how you'd react."

"Yeah, it sucks that she's related to the family undercutting your bids, but it's not like she did the actual bidding. And, damn, man. It's no secret how you feel about Colarusso Construction," Ben said. "You actually put her in a tough situation. If she told you, you'd be mad. If she didn't tell you, you'd be mad. There was no way out for her. No answer."

Well...hell.

He exhaled slowly and stared into the murky abyss below his feet. It was true. Still. "Lying is never the answer. Jinan kept her family a secret too. And look what happened." He ended up betrayed and alone.

"Ryder, listen to me." Ben set a hand his shoulder again. "Sophia is not Jinan. She did not choose her family over you and marry another man. You need to think back. Did you ever talk to her about Colarusso…I mean by name? Because you and I discussed them, but she wasn't there."

He rubbed his temple, trying to dispel the dull ache. "Yeah, I mentioned them to her when…" He paused, trying to recall when he'd actually said the name to her, and…*damn.* It was recent. The first time that came to mind was at the theater. The day before she left. "We were finished working on a set. Cathy told me I lost the ice cream parlor bid."

"Lost?" Ethan frowned. "Didn't you get that bid?"

He nodded. "I originally didn't, though. They called back the next day to offer it to…*son-of-a-bitch.*" His whole body stiffened as his heart dropped to his gut.

Ben grinned. "Looks like we have an *aha* moment."

"Care to share?" Ethan grinned too.

Ryder tossed the unopened beer back in the cooler and pushed to his feet. "I need to talk to Sophia," he said, heart pounding a little easier in a chest that was no longer tight with unrelenting fingers of betrayal. "Where did you say she was?"

Christ, he had some apologizing to do.

"At the theater. Where else?" Ben stood up and grinned. "I'm sure if you hurry, you can still catch her."

Ethan got to his feet. "If not, she rented a room at the resort."

His steps faltered, and he turned to face them. "Why? Is something wrong with Keiffer's place?"

No one told him about any issues.

"Yeah." Ben nodded. "I think she's having the same problem you're having with your house."

His heart took a hit, hard enough to make him blink. Memories of them together kept her from sleeping there?

A smile tugged his lips and he drew in another easy breath.

Maybe he hadn't screwed up so bad that things weren't fixable.

Yeah, he was an ass. He'd hurt her. And his insides were fisted tight with self-disgust. But he wasn't going to let it stop him from fighting for the woman he loved. Not this time. Not with Sophia. She was worth the effort. She was worth fighting for.

She was worth…everything. And he was going to do everything in his power to make it up to her.

If she'd have him back.

Chapter Nineteen

No matter how hard Sophia tried to concentrate on next month's production for Phoebe, she continued to stare at the white page in her sketch book. There was nothing to sketch because her mind was blank. Numb. Broken.

Like her heart.

Her spirit.

Wrinkling her nose, she grumbled, and refused to believe that. Refused to give up hope that Ryder would give her a chance to explain. They meant too much to each other not to—at least, he'd meant too much to her. She just hoped she'd somehow managed to get past his barriers and touch a piece of his heart.

What she wouldn't give to have a set to physically build right now. To throw herself into it. A way to work, but not think. Just do. Because thinking led to pain, and pain led to thoughts of Ryder.

She sucked in a ragged breath and blinked back a rogue round of tears. They weren't welcome. Not at work. In the shower, yes. In bed, yes. Not at work. She didn't do tears. She wasn't weak. She just missed him—so much.

Dammit.

Her eyes weren't blinking fast enough, so she wiped the escaping wetness from her face. Time to get up and get moving. A change of scenery. She grabbed her sketch pad and pencil, and headed to the main theater. Maybe if she sat in there and stared hard enough at the stage, inspiration would spark.

She'd never had this trouble before. Her mind usually swirled full of ideas. But yesterday and today, she just stared at her sketch pad.

It ticked her off.

No way did she want to let Phoebe down.

There were always the standard set designs, her mind reminded. But every director liked to put a slightly new spin on things, and Phoebe was no exception.

Because she was good. Smart.

Creative.

If Sophia's mind remained blank, she was going to have to ask Phoebe what she envisioned and go from there. Their thoughts were usually on the same page anyway.

Right now, though, hers were on Ryder, and how he'd stared at her through such a cold gaze on the sidewalk outside her apartment last week. A shiver raced down her spine at the memory.

Dammit.

She entered the main theater near the back by the stage and flicked on the lights, before walking up the center aisle. One by one, she counted the rows until she reached the fourth one. It was a good number. Especially that month. The fourth had been very inspiring.

With a sad chuckle, she sank into the first chair and stared out at the stage, but her broken mind was playing tricks on her, because she saw Ryder walk out. And everyone knew Ryder wasn't talking to her. Plus, he had no reason to be at the theater. Not to mentor. Not for work. Especially not for her.

"Sophia?"

She jumped. Her daydreams had never been this real. That even sounded like him.

Maybe this was her imagination's way of repairing itself, so she could work.

But when his gaze met hers and a familiar zing went through her, she sat up and blinked, squeezing the arms of the chair. Was that actually him?

He jumped off the stage and strode straight to her, and when she caught the scent of soap and cedar, with a hint of some kind of spice, her heart leapt in her tight chest.

"Ryder?"

Squatting down next to her chair in the aisle, he placed his hand over hers, all the while staring into her eyes. His were clear and unguarded, full of fear and hope. "I'm sorry," he said, voice surprisingly gentle. "I was an ass. I shouldn't have walked away from you."

"It's okay," she said, relieved to put it all behind them and work on moving forward.

But he set a finger to her lips, and shook his head. "No, it's not okay. I hurt you and I won't forgive myself for it. You've been nothing but sweet and kind and giving, and at the first sign of miscommunication I jumped to conclusions because of my past."

She knew he needed to get things off his chest. And she also knew, as he stroked her arm up and down, he was giving her his reassurance and strength, but he needed the connection, too, as if it was she who grounded him.

For several years he was closed up, kept things close to the vest. She knew this, but through his actions alone, she could tell he was trying to give her what he thought she needed. Dammit. He was making her insides melt. And her heart was swelling, and tears were filling her eyes, which she rapidly blinked away.

All she needed was his acceptance, and he was giving that to her, but she got the sense he needed to open up and get something off his chest. She continued to squeeze the arms of the chair—to keep from reaching for him—and remained silent to let him finish.

"During my second deployment to Iraq, I fell for a local girl, Jinan," he said, voice as steady as his gaze. "She left me to fulfill family duty by going through with an arranged marriage. For years I agonized over it. Wondered if I should've fought harder. Wondered if he was abusing her. Wondered why I wasn't enough for her to fight for. But there was this one time, over a very special New Year's Eve that a certain incredible woman managed to make me forget."

Sophia's heart raced so fast it nearly pounded itself out of her chest. "Me?"

"Yes. You." His gaze softened. "You got to me back then, Sophia. And you most definitely get to me now. But not only that, you *get* me. You understand

161

how I think. What I want. What I need. And I'll be honest, it scares the hell out of me. It fueled my misgivings last week. I know that's not an excuse, but I just wanted you to understand my issues and why I have them."

"Thanks for telling me. For letting me in," she said, reaching with her free hand to touch his scruffy jaw. "This thing between us scares me too, Ryder. But being with you makes me happy. And I like being happy."

"Happy looks good on you." He smiled into her palm. "I love making you happy. I love making you cry out my name when you come. I love being with you," he said, cupping her face. "But most importantly, I love you."

She sucked in a breath, and those damn tears returned. "I love you, too."

At this, he surged to his feet and pulled her with him. "You do?"

"Yes." She smiled, holding his face between her palms. "I love you."

He shifted closer and kissed her then, a happy and excited kiss at first, but then it slowed down to a deep, heartfelt journey of confirmation of everything they'd just admitted to one another. When they drew back for air, he tucked her head to his shoulder and held her tight.

As her breathing evened out, and her legs no longer threatened to buckle, she eased her grip on him and settled more comfortably against him. "I know it's crazy. It's only been a few weeks, but I feel what I feel." And she also felt his strong, reassuring heartbeat beneath her ear, and it empowered her to continue. "I'm sorry about my family, Ryder."

"Hey," he drew back, and dipped down to meet her gaze. "Don't be. You didn't do anything wrong. Neither did they. It's part of business."

"Actually, it wasn't." She filled him in on Gino's dealings, making sure he realized it wasn't anything her family's company would ever condone. And that she hadn't gone on more than that one date with the idiot. "So, once they fulfill the contracts he signed in the Poconos, Colarusso Construction will work New York territories."

He nodded. "I won't lie, that is good news. But, if I had to, I'd adjust. I'd figure something out."

"I know you would." She played with his collar, brushing his warm skin in the process. "You're a very resourceful guy."

"It takes the right inspiration. And you're it for me, Sophia." He slid his hands down her back to rest on her hips. "You make me happy, too. The way you look at me. The way your hands feel on me. The fact you even want to be with me...it all makes me happy."

"Good. I'm glad." She smiled, into his warm gaze.

"I realized something over the past few days," he said. "The thought of never having any of that with you again scares me much more than opening up and letting you in. I may have acted like an idiot, but I'm not stupid. I love you. I want you in my life. If I have to commute, I'll commute. I'll do whatever you want, whatever it takes to make this work."

She swallowed past her hot throat, feeling so light and happy she could float clear up to the beautiful ceiling he created. It was his thing. He created masterpieces. Created homes for families to enjoy. Businesses for people to thrive. He created a world of feeling and acceptance and strength for her that she never wanted to leave. "I love you, Ryder. So damn much."

"Can we give them a standing ovation now?"

The sound of Ben's voice made her jump. Ryder's hands tightened around her as they both turned to glance at the back of the theater where two Wyne brothers and their wives stood smiling at them.

"Sorry," he murmured. "Didn't know the peanut gallery followed me."

She slid her hands up around his neck and melted against him. "It's okay. I don't care who knows how I feel about you. I don't have anything to hide."

"Neither do I. In fact..." A slow, sexy smile stole across his face. "I like it best when there's nothing between us at all."

Epilogue

October arrived and brought with it changes in the leaves, temperature, sunset, and Sophia's life. Good changes. Great changes. Amazing changes.

The fall foliage was breathtaking. Cooler temperatures meant snuggling naked under a blanket with her own personal sexy furnace on a deck overlooking a spectacular lake. An early sunset led to naked snuggling under said blanket. Relocating to the Poconos ushered in new experiences, inspirations, a permanent job at Phoebe's theater, and unlimited naked blanket snuggling with Ryder. And knocking her designs out of the park for that major musical secured her very first Broadway set design job. Her friends were throwing her a celebration. Today.

"Proud of you," Ryder said, arms banded around her as he kissed her nose.

They stood inside a banquet hall at the resort where a celebration in her honor was underway. The Wynes were there, including Tyler who'd returned from his summer in Texas, and Mason and Jill who'd arrived back in town late last month. The vibe in the room was one of warmth and acceptance—just like being in Ryder's arms.

"Thank you." She spread her palms over his chest, kind of wishing they could skip to the part where they celebrated alone.

But she appreciated all the trouble her friends had gone through for her, and the fact her whole family drove in for the weekend. Ethan graciously offered up the vacant private Wyne townhouses, which her family was enjoying.

It warmed her heart how they welcomed Ryder from the start. She'd introduced them two months ago, and she wasn't sure what kind of initiation he had to pass with her brothers, but apparently, he'd nailed it. And the more her father saw of Ryder's work, the more impressed he became. Especially with the resort and the theater. He even offered him a job.

"You sure I can't persuade you to work for Colarusso?" her father asked again, stopping next to them with his arm around her mother. "We pride ourselves on excellent work, and I can see you would be a great fit."

Turning to face her parents, Ryder slid his arm around her waist and smiled. "Thank you, sir, but no. I appreciate that you believe I'm good enough for your company, but I am happy on my own."

Ryder confessed to her back in August that he'd researched Colarusso Construction and several of their jobs, and apologized for his misconception of their practices.

"And I am happy to be making the pierogi with your father later today." Her mother smiled, nodding toward Ryder's father, who stood across the room next to Lea while holding Melody. "Afterward, I am going to teach him my ravioli."

Sophia held back her gasp. Her mother never shared her secret recipe.

"Sounds like you're both in for a treat," Ryder said.

Her father patted his belly. "I know my stomach is."

They laughed, and after her parents moved on to talk to Phoebe's mother, who was sharing a toast with Ben's father, Sophia settled in closer to Ryder, feeling happy and blessed. Her niece and nephew giggled with Tyler as they jumped around. And she was really intrigued by the scowl on a certain off-duty officer's face as he watched Elle laughing at something her brother Tony said.

According to Elle, her research was almost done, and thankfully, "because the stubborn alpha was getting her on last nerve." Sophia could only imagine the tension inside the cruiser. Probably novel-worthy.

Later that afternoon, after the party ended, Sophia was happy to finally celebrate privately with Ryder. Nestled against him in a sleeping bag in the back of the truck, an unopened bottle of wine next to them, she stared out at the vista overlooking the valley. Wine, and scenery, and Ryder. Best way to celebrate. He'd whisked her away to their favorite, special spot, and ever the resourceful and thoughtful man, he backed the truck up, so they could watch the sunset from the bed.

"Thank you," he said, sitting with his back against the cab, arms wrapped around her while he kissed her head.

She turned to look at him. "For what? I should be thanking you for bringing me here. This is perfect."

"You're perfect. For me." His gaze was warm and open, and the way he was staring so deeply made her insides quiver. "When you first came back in June, I fought our connection. I didn't want to get involved, not because of my bullshit excuse that I wasn't looking for forever, but because I felt I had nothing to offer you. That I would let you down."

She reached out to touch his face. "You could never do that."

Remorse clouded his gaze. "Yes. I could." He kissed her palm. "I let my mother down. She asked me to go to the store, but I was too busy practicing ball, so she went instead, and died in a car accident."

"Oh, Ryder." Her heart squeezed in her chest. "That wasn't your fault. You know that, right?"

"Logically, yes. But not here." He grasped her hand and set it over his heart. "I could've prevented my mother from dying, and didn't. And I didn't prevent Jinan from marrying a man she didn't know. My track record with women I cared about sucked. I didn't want to add you to the list. I didn't want to not be there for you, too."

"But you are there, Ryder." She held his gaze, letting him see everything he meant to her. "You support and encourage. You're a blessing. You inspire me. Ground me. Make my heart pound. Make me whole."

"I know that now." A fierce, warm gleam entered his eyes, as he gently brushed her cheek with his thumb. "I realized what you needed was just me.

What you wanted was just me. And I was more than capable of delivering. In fact, I'd been giving you what you needed all along."

She smiled. "That's an understatement. You're very good at delivering."

His gaze turned teasing and he waggled his brow. "Yeah?"

"In that respect, too." She chuckled, running her hand down his abs, *the passion* running through her.

Cupping her face, he stared into her eyes as he slowly pressed her down on her back. "You're the love of my life, Sophia," he said, voice low and warm. "And the best damn thing to ever happen to me. Twice."

♥

If you enjoyed **WINE AND SCENERY**, *please consider leaving a review. Thank you.*

The fun began in Ben's story ***Wyne and Dine***, *and continues in* Mason's story, ***Wyne and Chocolate***, Ethan's story, ***Wyne and Song***, Lucas' story, ***Wine and Her New Year Cowboy***,
Noah's in ***Whine and Rescue***, Matt in **Wine and Hot Shoes**, Keiffer's story *(a Citizen Soldier/Harland County crossover novel)*, ***Her***

Troubled Cowboy, Nicco, Scott, and Jeremy, along with *a few others, will all get their stories, too, so don't miss the rest of the **Citizen Soldier Heroes**!*

*Read Brandi's story in **Her Uniform Cowboy***

Visit Donna Michaels' <u>website</u> at: www.DonnaMichaelsAuthor.com and sign up for her Newsletter. Enjoy exclusive reads, enter subscriber only contests, and be the first to know about upcoming books!

♥
Also by Donna Michaels

~The Citizen Soldier Series~
(Harland County Spinoff Series)

Wyne and Dine
Wyne and Chocolate
Wyne and Song
Wine and Her New Year Cowboy
Whine and Rescue (KW)
Wine and Hot Shoes
Wine and Scenery

~Harland County Series~

Harland County Christmas (Prequel)
Her Fated Cowboy
Her Unbridled Cowboy
Her Uniform Cowboy
Her Forever Cowboy
Her Healing Cowboy
Her Volunteer Cowboy
Her Indulgent Cowboy
Her Hell Yeah Cowboy (KW)
Her Troubled Cowboy (Citizen Soldier Crossover)
Her Hell No Cowboy (KW)

~The Men of At Ease Ranch Series~
~Entangled Publications~

In An Army Ranger's Arms
Her Secret Army Ranger
The Right Army Ranger
Army Ranger with Benefits
The Army Ranger's Surprise - 07/09/18

DonnaMichaelsAuthor.com

Connect with Donna Online

Donna's Facebook Profile:
https://www.facebook.com/DonnaMichaelsAuthor

Follow Donna on Twitter:
https://twitter.com/Donna_Michaels

Find Donna's Books on Goodreads:
http://www.goodreads.com/Donna_Michaels

Email: Donna_Michaels@msn.com

Website: www.DonnaMichaelsAuthor.com

To sign up for Donna's Newsletter go to:

http://tinyurl.com/zaxbqe6

Amazon:
http://www.amazon.com/Donna-Michaels/e/B008J24XR2/

Bookbub:
https://www.bookbub.com/authors/donna-michaels

About the Author

Donna Michaels Donna Michaels is an award winning, *New York Times & USA Today* bestselling author of *Romaginative* fiction. Her hot, humorous, and heartwarming stories include cowboys, men in uniform, and some sexy primal alphas who are equally matched by their heroines. With a husband recently retired from the military, a household of seven and several rescued cats, she never runs out of material. From short to epic, her books entertain readers across a variety of sub-genres, one was even hand-drawn into a Japanese translation. Published through Entangled Publications, The Wild Rose Press, Whimsical Publications, and self-published, she entertains readers across a variety of sub-genres, and one book is even being hand drawn into a Japanese translation....if only she could read it...

Bringing you HEAs-One Hot Alpha Hero at a Time

Thanks for reading,

~Donna

www.DonnaMichaelsAuthor.com

Made in the USA
Columbia, SC
11 April 2018